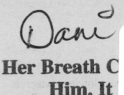 Dani

Her Breath C...
Him. It ...

"Slater?"

"Yeah, Kasey, it's me."

Years fell away. She felt seventeen again. Her knees shook as she moved closer and studied his face. Older, a few more lines. He was more rugged, his dark hair a little longer. Different, but so familiar.

"Aw, hell, Kasey." Slater shook his head as he opened his arms. "Come here, will you?"

With a nervous laugh, she moved into his arms. Tears gathered in her eyes and she blinked them back. He was solid muscle against her, his scent masculine. His touch made her dizzy. How could he have this effect on her after all these years?

She'd obviously never gotten over him. How could she protect her heart a second time around?

Dear Reader,

February, month of valentines, celebrates lovers—which is what Silhouette Desire does *every* month of the year. So this month, we have an extraspecial lineup of sensual and emotional page-turners. But how do you choose which exciting book to read first when all six stories are asking *Be Mine?*

Bestselling author Barbara Boswell delivers February's MAN OF THE MONTH, a gorgeous doctor who insists on being a full-time father to his newly discovered child, in *The Brennan Baby. Bride of the Bad Boy* is the wonderful first book in Elizabeth Bevarly's brand-new BLAME IT ON BOB trilogy. Don't miss this fun story about a marriage of inconvenience!

Cupid slings an arrow at neighboring ranchers in *Her Torrid Temporary Marriage* by Sara Orwig. Next, a woman's thirtieth-birthday wish brings her a supersexy cowboy—and an unexpected pregnancy—in *The Texan*, by Catherine Lanigan. Carole Buck brings red-hot chemistry to the pages of *Three-Alarm Love*. And Barbara McCauley's *Courtship in Granite Ridge* reunites a single mother with the man she'd always loved.

Have a romantic holiday this month—and every month— with Silhouette Desire. Enjoy!

Melissa Senate

Melissa Senate
Senior Editor

Please address questions and book requests to:
Silhouette Reader Service
U.S.: 3010 Walden Ave., P.O. Box 1325, Buffalo, NY 14269
Canadian: P.O. Box 609, Fort Erie, Ont. L2A 5X3

BARBARA McCAULEY
COURTSHIP IN GRANITE RIDGE

SILHOUETTE *Desire*®
Published by Silhouette Books
America's Publisher of Contemporary Romance

SILHOUETTE BOOKS

ISBN 0-373-76128-7

COURTSHIP IN GRANITE RIDGE

Printed in U.S.A.

Books by Barbara McCauley

Silhouette Desire

Woman Tamer #621
Man From Cougar Pass #698
Her Kind of Man #771
Whitehorn's Woman #803
A Man Like Cade #832
Nightfire #875
*Texas Heat #917
*Texas Temptation #948
*Texas Pride #971
Midnight Bride #1028
The Nanny and the Reluctant Rancher #1066
Courtship in Granite Ridge #1128

*Hearts of Stone

BARBARA McCAULEY

was born and raised in California, and has spent a good portion of her life exploring the mountains, beaches and deserts so abundant there. The youngest of five children, she grew up in a small house, and her only chance for a moment alone was to sneak into the backyard with a book and quietly hide away.

With two children of her own now and a busy household, she still finds herself slipping away to enjoy a good novel. A daydreamer and incurable romantic, she says writing has fulfilled her most incredible dream of all—breathing life into the people in her mind and making them real. She has one loud and demanding Amazon parrot named Fred and a German shepherd named Max. When she can manage the time, she loves to sink her hands into fresh-turned soil and make things grow.

One

"Hugh Slater, you need to git yerself a woman."

With a silent groan, Slater kept his nose buried in his newspaper and ignored Digger Jones, hoping that the silver-bearded owner of the Hungry Bear Café would move on to badger another customer. It had been a long, hot day, and all Slater wanted to do was catch up on a week's worth of mail and newspapers and eat his meal in peace.

No such luck.

"Did you hear me, son?" Digger slid the blue plate special—a two-inch thick T-bone with mashed potatoes smothered in home-style gravy—across the Formica-topped table and slapped down a plate of steaming biscuits. "I said you need to git yerself a woman."

"Didn't see them on the menu," Slater replied dryly, keeping his attention on his paper as he reached for a biscuit.

"Don't you wisecrack me in my own establishment,

boy.'' Digger straightened his remarkably fit seventy-two-year-old, six-foot-three frame and sniffed indignantly. "You might be bigger and younger than me, but I can still whoop your butt. Just giving a little friendly advice, that's all.''

Everyone in Cactus Flat knew that one of Digger's meals always came with advice or criticism, most often both. They also knew—as did Digger—that there was no place to get a better steak or apple cobbler in all of West Texas. And since Slater had his eye on a piece of that cobbler after his meal, he knew when to keep his mouth shut.

Digger, on the other hand, didn't.

"'Bout time you settled down, son.'' Digger ignored the ring of the cook's bell that the next order was up. "What are you, thirty-two, thirty-three?''

"Thirty-four.'' Not that it mattered, Slater thought irritably. He had no intention of "settling down.'' Not now. Not ever. Even the ten months he'd been here in Cactus Flat working as foreman on the Stone Creek Oil rigs was a record for him. He was feeling anxious lately, restless. He knew it was time to move on and had already accepted a new job in Alaska on a rig there. Stone Creek Oil was on a month hiatus after ten months of nonstop drilling on four rigs, and Slater figured now was as good a time as any to leave. He'd planned on telling Jared Stone today, but Jared, who was not only his boss, but also his friend, wasn't going to like it.

"Thirty-four? That old, huh?'' Digger shook his head pitifully. "Man your age needs a sweet young thing and a passel of kids to come home to every night.''

Slater frowned and glanced at Digger over the top of his newspaper. "I don't see a ring on your hand.''

"Exactly my point.'' Digger emphasized his statement

by pointing a long, thick-knuckled finger. "I spent my life prospecting one claim after another, moving from one mine to the next, just like you with your oil wells. I was a damned fool. Don't want to see the same thing happen to you, boy, that's all."

"Hey, Cupid, you gonna jack the jaw all night?" Floyd Perkins bellowed from the corner booth. "A man could grow old waitin' for a cup a coffee 'round here."

"Somethin' wrong with your legs, Perkins?" Digger hollered back. "Slater and me are having a conversation."

"Sounds more like you're the one having the conversation," Floyd grumbled. "Why don't you leave that poor boy to read his paper and eat his meal in peace?"

"What paper you reading that's so dang interesting?" Digger squinted and leaned close. "The *Granite Ridge Gazette*. Why in tarnation you readin' that? Granite Ridge is five hundred miles from here."

Slater ground his back teeth together. He should have known better than to expect any privacy here. What he read and why was his business, and he had no intention of sharing that business with anyone—especially Digger Jones.

"You know somebody there?" Digger kept on. "I hear they got some fine horse ranches down that way, especially quarter horses. Joe Stovall bought two cutters from a fellow named—" he rubbed thoughtfully at his chin "—hell, what *was* his name...Jack something..."

Slater braced himself.

The cook's bell rang persistently, cutting off Digger's train of thought. He turned sharply and growled at the intrusion. "All right, already. I'm coming. Stop yer clanging."

With a sigh of relief, Slater watched Digger shuffle

off, then settled back into the booth, struggling to fit his long legs under the tabletop. He stared at the paper in front of him, at the familiar names and faces.

Granite Ridge.

For the past ten years, since he'd left his hometown, the *Gazette* had followed him across the country: Oklahoma, New Mexico, Washington and now back to Texas. The only time he hadn't received the paper was during his stint in Venezuela. The rig he'd been working on there had been too remote to receive mail with any dependability, so he'd let it lapse those months, then immediately started it up again when he'd returned to the States. Whether for some morbid kind of punishment— a reminder of all the things he could never have, that he never did have—simple curiosity or just plain habit, he didn't know or care.

Thankful that Digger was busy harassing Pete Walker for his lack of attendance at the last town meeting, Slater scooped up a forkful of mashed potatoes and turned his attention back to the front page of his paper. The top stories of the past week were Mary Lou Hebbit's—assisted by her husband, Bobby Joe Hebbit—giving birth to twin girls in the flatbed of a hay truck, and the Hackett brothers' assigned twenty hours' community service for being drunk and disorderly.

Slater seemed to recall a few nights that he'd spent with Bobby and Billy Hackett himself. The brothers had played in the bars as hard as they'd worked on their daddy's farm, but always showed up for church on Sundays and were the first to volunteer for the town's annual Ladies' Auxiliary carnival and auction. If anyone needed to "git himself a woman," Slater thought with a smile, it was definitely those boys.

He skimmed the city council and agriculture reports,

then paused at the wedding section, which had one entry: Millie Johnson and Todd Overby were engaged and getting married in two weeks. Millie and Todd? Slater shook his head as he took a sip of coffee. They'd practically been babies when he'd left. How could they be old enough to get married?

With a sigh, he moved on to the obituaries, thankful at least, that column was empty. He took another sip of coffee and started to fold the paper when the bottom of the last page, an assortment of classified ads and personals, caught his attention.

Wanted: One Husband. Not too old. Must like kids. List good qualities. Call Kasey at the Double D Ranch—555-4832 or send picture to 684 Marva Lane, Granite Ridge, TX.

He nearly choked. Coffee sloshed over the sides of his cup as he slammed it down.

Kasey...as in Kasey Donovan?

He shook off the coffee he'd spilled onto his paper and looked at the ad again. Good God! He *had* read it right. It was Kasey.

Kasey Donovan had been his sister Jeanie's best friend since they'd been six. They'd been inseparable. Kasey, with her wild red hair, vibrant green eyes and a ready-to-take-on-the-world attitude, had been a sharp contrast to Jeanie's silky blond hair, pale blue eyes and quiet acceptance of whatever life dealt her. Which, Slater thought with a tightening in his gut, had been one lousy hand after another. She'd learned young that life wasn't fair. They both had.

He missed her. God, how he missed her.

He let the pain roll through him, then shook it off and

stared at the newspaper again. Kasey Donovan. With her bright laugh and enthusiasm for life, she emerged from a dark past like a rainbow after the storm.

He'd lost track of her after he'd left Granite Ridge, though he had read that after she'd graduated high school she'd married some hotshot journalist and moved to New York. Obviously if she was looking for a husband, that hadn't worked out. Then four years later her mother had died after a long illness, six months after that, her father from a heart attack. Slater had been in Venezuela at the time and hadn't heard until he'd gotten back to the States. By the time he'd called, the phone had been disconnected.

The Donovans had been like some kind of a TV family. Always there for each other, loving...accepting. Mrs. Donovan had been the mother Jeanie had lost when she was two, and, Slater recalled with a smile, Mr. and Mrs. Donovan had both treated him as a son, too. Kasey's mother would always insist he stay for dinner every time he came to pick up Jeanie, then afterward Mr. Donovan would discuss the latest issue of *Rancher's Digest* over a cup of strong black coffee, asking Slater his opinion or advice on horse breeding.

Something Slater's own father had never done.

The Donovans had been Slater's only regret when he'd left Granite Ridge. His only regret even still.

And now Kasey was advertising for a husband?

He shook his head at the thought. Kasey. His little Kasey. He'd taught her how to ride a bike, helped her with her science homework. At fifteen she'd been all arms and legs and a mouthful of braces. At seventeen, when he'd left, she'd emerged a young woman with curves that had every male drooling and every female turning a lovely shade of green.

And now, here he was, ten years later.

And here was Kasey.

Obviously she was in a serious situation if she was advertising for a husband. But whatever her problem might be, there had to be another solution than marrying a stranger.

"Slater!" Digger's loud exclamation from the other side of the diner brought Slater's head up. "Jack Slater, from the Bar S. That was that big rancher's name."

Slater's back stiffened at the name he hadn't said in ten years.

Coffeepot in hand, Digger moved beside the booth and refilled Slater's cup. "Hey, he must be a kin of yours. Brother, maybe? Cousin?"

Digger had a hold of the bone now, and Slater knew the old man wouldn't let go. So let him have it. What difference did it make?

"Father," Slater said evenly, and took a sip of coffee.

"No kidding." Digger whistled. "And all this time we thought you had no family."

I don't, Slater thought. Not with Jack Slater, anyway.

Ignoring Digger's rattling on about fathers and sons, Slater stared at Kasey's ad again. Jeanie's death had been as hard on Kasey as it had him. He'd walked out on her ten years ago and let her down. He had an opportunity to make up for that now.

Right or wrong, mistake or not, he was going back. Even if it meant he'd have to see Jack Slater again.

Something very strange was going on.

It wasn't just the stares she'd gotten at the market in town, Kasey thought as she pulled her pickup off the main road and headed down the gravel drive that led to her house. There'd been sidelong glances and raised eye-

brows, too. And Kasey would swear that June Binder-
meyer had actually snickered when she'd bagged the groceries.

Very strange.

What could have happened in the two weeks she and
her sons had been gone? She'd taken the last of the boys'
summer vacation and gone to Dallas to look for a brood-
mare, the first of what she hoped would eventually be a
full stable of quarter horses. She'd looked at a dozen
mares in the first three days and had finally settled on a
beautiful sorrel from the Circle Q named Miss Lucy. The
animal was more than Kasey could afford, but one look
and she was lost. She'd bought her and made arrangements for her to be delivered in a few days, then immediately placed an ad for a stud in several papers, including the *Granite Ridge Gazette*.

But placing an ad for a stud was no reason for anyone
to look at her oddly, Kasey thought with a frown. This
was horse country. Still, at the post office when she'd
picked up the bag with her mail and papers, disapproval
had been plainly etched on Mildred Macklin's face. And
was it Kasey's imagination, or had Mildred actually
slammed her window shut when Steven, Mildred's son,
had come over to say hello?

Very, very strange.

Shaking her head, Kasey shut off the engine and
looked down at her sleeping sons. Cody, her eight-year-
old, and Troy, almost seven, were slumped into each
other, making it hard to tell where Cody's thick, dark
hair stopped and Troy's wavy auburn hair started. It had
been a long, busy two weeks for them. After the horse
business was taken care of, they'd gone to the amusement
park in Arlington, the rodeo in Dallas and the water park
outside of Fort Worth.

It didn't matter to her that she couldn't afford it. Her sons deserved a family vacation, a *real* family vacation, not an assignment that their father dragged them along on, then left them all in a hotel while he went off to do his research.

Cody sat up abruptly, realizing the car had stopped. "Are we home?" he asked, blinking several times.

Home. They'd only moved here from New York two months ago, and the word *home* had never had a nicer sound. She smiled and combed her fingers through his hair. "We are."

Cody realized at the moment that his younger brother was sleeping on him. "Get off me," he said, shoving Troy away.

Troy rubbed at his eyes and yawned. "We home?"

"Mom," Cody whined in disgust. "Troy drooled on me."

"Did not."

"Did, too."

"You're a moron."

"You're an idiot."

"Am not."

"Are, too. Idiot, idiot."

"That's enough." Kasey helped both boys out of the truck and sent them each a sharp look. Ah, yes, home, she thought with a sigh. Back to normal.

"Mom," Cody said, putting the disagreement behind him and moving forward. "Can Troy and me go over to Brian's house? We wanna show him the Battle Boy and Maniac Man we got on vacation."'

"It's Troy and I." She reached into the bed of the truck, then shoved a bag of groceries into each boy's arms before grabbing two herself. "And not today. It's already starting to get dark, and you both still need to unpack.''

Cody and Troy started to argue with her, but she held firm and herded them through the front door and into the kitchen. She glanced at the answering machine on the kitchen wall phone, amazed at the number that was lit up on the display. Fifteen? Had her ad for a stud been that successful? She'd expected maybe five or six calls, but fifteen? She'd also noticed that her bag of mail had been stuffed to overflowing. Were there that many letters, also?

She'd deal with the messages and mail later. Right now she needed to get her food put away and her sons fed. They'd started arguing again, with Cody calling Troy a drool-mouth and Troy calling Cody a jerk. It would come to fists soon if she didn't intercede, and she was too tired to deal with blood right now.

Separating them once again, the groceries were nearly put away when there was a knock at the front door. Like a call to dinner, both boys charged toward the sound.

Kasey frowned. She wasn't expecting anyone, though it might be Sandy, Brian's mother. She'd been caring for the horses and watching the house for Kasey while she was away. But Sandy thought they were coming home in the morning, not tonight.

She slid the last half gallon of milk into the refrigerator and shut the door, suddenly aware of the absolute quiet.

"Cody? Troy?"

When she came around the corner, she saw them standing just inside the screen door, staring at the ceiling. No, not the ceiling, she realized as she moved toward them. They were staring at a person. A very *tall* person she couldn't make out through the screen door.

"Can I help you?" she asked, feeling a little nervous

at the sheer size of the denim-clad stranger at her door. She tried to make out his face, but a black cowboy hat and the dim light shadowed his features. Though she was used to and didn't mind being a single mom, at times like this she at least wished she owned a dog.

"Acacia Donovan?" a deep, strangely familiar voice asked.

Acacia? No one ever called her that. No one except...

Heart pounding, Kasey flipped on the porch light. He took off his hat and grinned down at her.

Her breath caught. It couldn't be. It wasn't possible. *Slater.*

Ten years fell away. She suddenly felt that her arms and legs were too long, her braces too tight, her hair too curly and her voice too high.

"Slater?" she whispered.

He nodded. "Yeah, Kasey, it's me."

Her knees shook as she moved closer to the screen door and studied his face. Older, a few more lines. He was more rugged, his dark hair a little longer. Different, but so familiar.

"You gonna make me stand out here all night?" he asked.

She looked down at her sons, who were still frozen in place, their necks bent back, their mouths open as they stared at the stranger. Under a different situation, she might have laughed. Unless they were sleeping, her sons were never quiet this long. But this wasn't just a different situation.

This was Slater.

Her fingers shook as she reached for the screen door and pushed it open. Slater glanced down at Cody and Troy. Still staring, the boys slowly parted, and he stepped inside.

Kasey's first impulse was to yell for Jeanie, to tell her that her big brother was here to pick her up. Her second impulse was to jump into his arms. She did neither. All she could do was stand there, a lump in her throat and a tight ache in her chest.

"Ah, these are my sons," she said finally. "Cody—" she touched her oldest son's head "—and Troy. Boys, this is Slater, an old friend of mine."

Troy pressed against her, curious, but cautious, while Cody craned his neck upward and stared. "How old *are* you?" Cody asked.

"Cody Thomas Morgan," Kasey reprimanded, "where are your manners?

"Well, *you* said he was old," Cody grumbled.

With a half grin, Slater slipped his hat back on, then knelt and leaned close to Cody. "I'm thirty-four," he whispered. "Is that old?"

Cody shrugged. "Not so bad. My mom's twenty-seven."

Slater raised his brows in mock surprise. "That old, huh? Do you have to help her across the street and speak real loud so she can hear you?"

Cody and Troy both burst into giggles. Kasey rolled her eyes and shook her head. What in the world was all this talk about age? Cody had never asked anyone how old they were before.

"We just got back from vacation," Cody offered. "My mom bought a new horse called Miss Lucy, and we got to go to the rodeo and the water park."

"And ride a roller coaster," Troy added. He'd unglued himself from her side and had moved a few inches closer to the visitor.

"You ever take your kids on a roller coaster?" Cody asked.

"Cody," Kasey warned, though she was curious herself now, "that's enough questions."

Slater smiled. "I don't have any kids."

"How come?" Suspicion edged Cody's voice. "Don't you like them?"

"Cody! I said, that's enough." Kasey took hold of her son's shoulders.

"Sure, I like kids." Slater tipped his hat back and looked at both Cody and Troy. "But I was moving around a lot, working on oil wells, and I just never got married."

Cody's eyes widened. "You work on oil wells. That's cool. Does oil really squirt ten miles up and get all—"

Kasey clamped a hand over her son's mouth. "No more questions. I'd like to talk to Slater now if it's all right with you two."

Cody and Troy glanced at each other and smiled. "Sure, Mom," Cody said, looking back up at her. "You want us to leave you guys alone?"

Leave them alone? Kasey frowned at her son. Why was everyone, including her sons, acting so odd today? Was there a full moon tonight? "That's not necessary."

Slater straightened. "I, uh, heard you got married."

She wondered how a man who'd walked away from family and friends—without so much as a glance backward—could have heard anything. "I'm divorced. Two years now."

They stared at each other, the momentary silence awkward and heavy. Then they both spoke at the same time.

"You look—"

"You've sure—"

They both stopped, then smiled.

"Aw, hell, Kasey." Slater shook his head as he opened his arms. "Come here, will you?"

With a small laugh, she moved into his arms. He was solid muscle against her, his scent masculine, his touch so familiar. This really *was* Slater. Tears gathered in her eyes and she blinked them back, afraid that he might see them and think her silly or childish.

Smiling, she pulled away and looked up at him. His eyes were still the same deep brown, but there were lines beside them now. She frowned at the jagged scar on his right temple and wondered what had happened. His jaw was more square, his chin stronger, his hair a richer, darker brown.

When she was seventeen she'd thought him the handsomest man alive. Looking at him now, her opinion was still the same.

His arms around her, his hands touching her waist made her dizzy. How could he have this effect on her after all these years? He couldn't. She was overtired, stressed from her trip. Why else would her pulse be racing and her head ringing?

"You gonna get that?"

"What?"

He nodded toward the kitchen. "The phone. It's ringing."

"Oh, yes." She heard it now. "Of course."

She pulled away and backed toward the kitchen. "Cody, Troy, take Slater into the living room and keep him company. I'll be right back."

Slater watched Kasey turn and disappear into the kitchen. He glanced around the entry, letting the past back into his life for a moment. Everything was the same; the dark oak table just inside the screen door where Mrs. Donovan had always kept fresh flowers, the hat rack beside it where Mr. Donovan had always hung his gray Stetson beside his blue baseball cap. And the family portrait, taken on the front porch, not long before he'd left. He took a step closer and grinned at the framed snapshot. Kasey, with her brilliant smile and wild red hair, one arm looped over her father's broad shoulders, the other arm twined around her mother's slender waist. He stared at the picture and his smile faded.

The same, and yet, not the same.

He glanced down at Kasey's sons. Definitely not the same.

He was still trying to sort everything, but nothing seemed to fit into place. He didn't know what he'd expected, but he certainly hadn't expected what he'd found. She'd grown up. *Really* grown up, he thought, recalling the soft swell of her breasts under the pink cotton knit shirt she wore. Her eyes were bigger than he'd remembered, the green darker. Before, she'd always worn her mass of red hair in a ponytail or pinned up. Now, long auburn curls framed her heart-shaped face and emphasized her high cheeks and wide, sensuous lips.

Sensuous? Had he really thought that about Kasey? He wanted to kick himself. Kasey's sons were staring up at him, their expressions serious, as if they'd heard every unspoken thought. Feeling guilty, Slater looked away and shifted uncomfortably.

"You come here to see my mom?" Cody asked.

It was the older boy who'd asked the question, Slater realized. Cody. He nodded to the child. "That's right."

"Why?"

Slater raised his brows, then knelt in front of the boys. "We used to be friends."

"Aren't you anymore?

Good question, Slater thought. "I hope so."

Cody seemed to think about that for a moment. The younger boy, Troy, moved closer and stared intently.

"That's a neat scar," Troy said, finding his voice. "Would you like to marry our mom?"

Slater doubted that a two-by-four across his head could have hit him harder. Were things that bad with Kasey that her own sons were interviewing potential husbands for her? Speechless, he stared at the two boys. They stood in front of him, their eyes locked on his, waiting for an answer. He didn't want to hurt their feelings, or offend Kasey, but the fact was, he had no intention of marrying anyone. He liked his life just fine as it was.

Slater ran his fingers through his hair. "Well, I...it's like this, boys, I, uh, think your mom's great and all, but—"

"The nerve of some people!"

Slater nearly fell backward at Kasey's sudden exclamation. She stood at the kitchen doorway, arms folded tightly. Slater stood abruptly, bumping into the entryway table.

"It's nothing, personal, Kasey, I just—"

"Nothing personal?" She moved into the room, her eyes flashing. "Nothing *personal?* Of course, it's personal!"

"I'm sorry, Kase, I just don't—"

"Why should you be sorry?" She threw her arms out, then jammed them onto her slim hips. "I place an ad for a simple business deal, and all the guy cares about is my financial statement and bloodlines."'

Financial statement? Bloodlines? Slater felt his own blood begin to boil. Kasey Donovan came from the finest people that were ever born, and as far as financial statements were concerned, if some slime-jerk wanted money to marry Kasey, then he wasn't fit to be in the same room with her. Hell, the same state even!

Is that all this was to her? A business deal? Thank God

he'd gotten here before she'd done anything stupid. He had to make her see that she couldn't go ahead with this ridiculous scheme.

"Kasey—" Slater looked at Cody and Troy "—could I talk to you, uh, privately?"

Still frowning, Kasey stared at Slater for a moment, then snapped out of her tirade. "Oh, of course. Cody, Troy, go get your suitcases out of the car and unpack while I talk to Slater."

They started to argue, but one look, a look only a mother can perfect, had both boys turning away, shoulders slumped.

"Come, on, Slate." She turned and walked back to the kitchen. "Give a hand while I get dinner started. You're staying, of course."

Just like the old days, he thought with a smile and followed. But when she bent to search through a stack of cans in the corner pantry, Kasey's well-rounded bottom encased in snug jeans reminded him this was definitely not the old days, and she definitely was not the same Kasey.

Clearing his throat, he looked away and studied a blue-framed needlepoint by the back door that said, Home Is Where The Heart Is.

"Here—" she tossed him a can of green beans then headed for the refrigerator "—open these while I mix the hamburgers. So you're into oil now, huh? Where you working?"

He caught the can and turned to the electric opener on the counter beside the sink. "I've got a job starting on an Alaskan rig in three weeks."

"Alaska!" Hamburger in one hand and an onion in the other, Kasey closed the refrigerator door with a bump of her hip. "You hate the cold. Remember the ski trip we took to Colorado? You were miserable the whole time.''

He didn't exactly hate it, he just preferred the heat. And this was getting way off the subject he wanted to pursue. ''Look, Kasey, about your ad in the paper—''

''You saw it?'' She closed the refrigerator and stared at him in amazement. ''How?''

He wasn't quite ready to explain that he'd subscribed to the *Granite Ridge Gazette* for the past ten years. Ignoring her question, he clipped the can of green beans onto the opener, turned it on, and glanced over his shoulder at her. ''Kase, there are always options.''

Still holding the package of hamburger in her hand, she stared blankly at him. ''Options?''

''Alternatives, another way to, uh, deal with your situation.''

She frowned. ''Well, I suppose there are, but I really haven't the time or money for anything else. Besides, the good old-fashioned way is more my style. At least this way, if it doesn't work, I can get my money back.''

Slater's hand slipped off the electric can opener and the can clattered onto the counter.

''Get your money back?'' he rasped. ''You mean to tell me you're actually going to *pay* someone to marry you?''

Two

Kasey blinked. A slow opening and closing of her lids, as if, in the space between dark and light, Slater's words might actually make some sense.

Pay someone to marry her?

What, on God's good earth, was he talking about?

All she could do was stare, despite the fact that green beans were running over the counter and into the sink, despite the fact that Slater was waiting for her to say something.

Had he slipped in a puddle of oil and fallen off a derrick? Or maybe a loose coupling had knocked him in the head. Maybe that scar on his forehead had been a more serious injury than it appeared.

She cleared her throat and met his dark, intense gaze. "Excuse me?"

He frowned. "Look, Kasey, I know it's none of my business. You're obviously a big girl now. But advertising for a husband in a newspaper is just not safe. God only knows what kind of maniac might show up at your door.''

A maniac *did* show up at her door, she thought in disbelief. Him. "Slater," she said quietly, "could you, uh, explain to me exactly why you're here?"

"Kasey, look—" he sighed deeply "—I realize life gets a little lonely. Sometimes when things overwhelm a person, they don't think too clearly and they make rash decisions.''

"You mean my decision to *buy* a husband," she said, wanting to make sure she understood him. Only she didn't understand him.

"You gotta admit, Kase, it is a little crazy."

Crazy? He was talking to her about *crazy?* She looked at the package of meat in her hand. Did he really think that she wanted to buy a husband, like she might a pound of hamburger? Where in the world did he get such an idea?

"This advertisement," she asked carefully, "exactly where did you see it?"

"It doesn't matter where I saw it," he said firmly. "I just thought that maybe you needed someone, a friend. With your parents gone, and you being divorced and having a family…" His voice trailed off, and he shifted anxiously.

Family. Her sons. Kasey suddenly realized they'd been awfully quiet for awfully long. She glanced at the kitchen door and saw two little heads duck away, then heard the sound of footsteps heading up the stairs.

If this day got any stranger, she'd be in the twilight zone.

Maybe she *was* in the twilight zone. She remembered the looks she'd gotten in town, the snickers, the way

Mildred had treated her when Steven had wanted to say hello.

The way her sons had acted with Slater.

Could it be...was it possible?

"Excuse me for a minute, will you?" She shoved the hamburger at Slater. "I'll be right back."

"But—"

She ignored him and headed straight for her sons' bedroom. She had the strangest—and most horrible—feeling that they knew something she didn't.

She found them putting their clothes away, exactly as she'd told them to do. That cinched it. If they were actually doing as she'd asked, without being told three times, there was no doubt they were up to something.

They glanced at her when she entered the room, but continued unpacking with the same attention they might give a video game.

"Hey, Mom." Cody pulled a stack of baseball cards out of his suitcase and shuffled them nervously. "Is Mr. Slater still here?"

"As a matter of fact, he is." She closed the door quietly behind her, then leaned back against it. They'd break, she knew, and based on the tension in the room, it wouldn't be long.

"Is he gonna stay?" Troy asked, then bit his bottom lip when Cody shot him a vicious look.

"Stay?" Kasey repeated. "Would there be a reason why he might stay?"

"He's your friend, isn't he?" Cody dropped the baseball cards into a big box along with all the other cards in his collection, then glanced at his mother, his look hopeful.

"A friend I haven't seen in ten years," Kasey said. "And now, suddenly, here he is, telling me the most amazing story about an ad in a newspaper. Something about a husband.''

The boys looked at each other, then Cody hurriedly turned his attention back to unpacking his suitcase. Troy carefully studied one of the rocks he'd collected on the trip.

''The funny thing is,'' Kasey went on, ''I don't seem to remember placing an ad in any newspaper for a husband. I mean, I could have forgotten, being so busy with the trip and all, but I don't think so.'' She moved closer to her sons and stood over them, arms folded. ''What do you boys think?''

Cody grabbed a handful of dirty socks and started for the dresser. Kasey stepped around him, then pointed to his bed. ''Sit.'' She looked at Troy. ''You, too.''

Eyes downcast, both boys sat.

Arms folded, she stood over her sons. ''You want to tell me something?''

Cody sighed. ''We were gonna tell ya, really, but we sorta forgot.''

''You forgot?''

''Yeah,'' Troy agreed. ''We forgot.''

She raised one brow. ''Tell me *exactly* what you forgot.''

Cody looked at Troy, then slumped his shoulders in defeat. ''Well, you know when we were on vacation, after you bought Miss Lucy from Mr. Murdock, and Troy and me were playing checkers?''

''Cody was cheating,'' Troy piped in.

''Was not.'' Cody scowled at his brother. ''You just don't know how to play.''

''Do, too.'' Troy screwed up his face. ''Mom taught me.''

"That's enough." She remembered now. They'd been arguing over the game then, as well. "Go on, Cody."

Cody threw Troy one last look, then turned back to his mother. "Well, when we asked you to play, too, you said you would, as soon as you finished what you were doing and we asked you what you were doing and you said you were writing an ad and we asked you what for and you said you were looking for a horse husband for Miss Lucy."

It took a moment for Cody's rush of words to pull together. The hotel room in Dallas. Cody and Troy had been asking her questions about the ad and Miss Lucy. She hadn't quite been ready to explain the process of hiring a studhorse, and somehow the term "horse husband" just sort of popped out. In any case, she still wasn't quite connecting the dots here. "And?"

"Well, Troy and me, well, me really, 'cause Troy don't read so good yet—"

"So well," Kasey corrected out of habit.

"Yeah, so we were looking at one of the newspapers you brought along on the trip, you know, the *Granite Ridge Gazette*, and there was a place you can buy and sell things, so that's what we did."

"What did you do?" she asked, breath held.

"You know, we wrote an ad for you."

Oh, dear Lord, they didn't...

Cody's grin was as wide as it was proud. "Filled it out and mailed it, all by ourselves. We were going to surprise you."

She stared at her sons, unable to speak. *Surprise her?* That was the understatement of the century.

Knees weak, Kasey sank slowly onto the bed opposite her sons and closed her eyes. It would certainly explain

the bizarre way everyone had treated her in town, Slater
showing up, all the mail and phone messages—

Oh, no...that must be why she had so many calls. They
were for stud services *and* potential husbands. She nearly
choked at the juxtaposition of the two.

Her eyes flew open. "Cody," she asked slowly, "exactly what did this ad say?"

"Not much." He reached behind him into his suitcase,
then pulled out a piece of paper and handed it to her. "It
don't cost as much if you don't use a lotta words. Troy
and me saved some money you gave us from the video
arcade."

The supreme sacrifice, Kasey realized, not even bothering to correct her son's grammar this time. She took
the slip of paper as if it were a snake, then drew in a
deep breath and read, "Wanted: One Husband. Not too
old. Must like kids. List good qualities. Call Kasey at the
Double D Ranch—555-4832 or send picture to 684
Marva Lane, Granite Ridge, TX."

Her heart stopped, then raced. *No. This wasn't happening. It couldn't be.* The words blurred as she stared
at the paper.

Cody looked down at the floor and kicked at the edge
of the blue braided rug between the twin beds. "We
know Daddy made you cry when he went to Mexico with
Gloria, so we thought maybe...well, you know, that you
might feel better if you weren't alone anymore."

Kasey felt her breath catch in the back of her throat.
She'd been so careful to hide her emotions from her sons
when Paul had walked out on them. How could she have
explained to a then four- and six-year-old that the tears
she'd shed had been anger and frustration at herself? Certainly not because she was alone, or because she missed
their father.

She'd made it on her own for the past two years and she was proud of that. She *wanted* to be single now. She enjoyed the independence. All she needed was her sons and this ranch. Nothing else in the world mattered to her.

She looked at them now. They were watching her, waiting for her approval. How could she be upset with them? They wanted her to be happy and they thought a husband—any husband—would make her happy. She shook her head. They had so much to learn.

"Cody. Troy." She knelt on the floor and leaned in close to her sons. "I'm not alone, sweethearts. I have you both. Don't you know how much I love you, and how happy it makes me to be here with you, living in Grandma and Grandpa's house? We won't have to move anymore, and you won't have to change schools or make new friends all the time."

"Brian says Miss Foster, the first-grade teacher is nice." Troy rolled the rock he held back and forth between his hands. "He said he was in her class two years ago and on Fridays she lets kids bring in stuff to share. I'm going to bring my rock collection."

Kasey smiled. Troy's rock collection was his pride and joy. He'd been gathering up pebbles and stones in a shoe box for the past two years. Since Paul had left.

"Won't you and Brian be in the same class?" Kasey turned to her older son.

"We're gonna sit next to each other." Cody pulled at the frayed edges of the growing hole on the knee of his jeans. "He says his dad is taking him on a camping trip next weekend and me and Troy could come along."

In that instant, Kasey understood so much more than what her sons were saying. Maybe even more than they understood. They weren't just looking for a husband for her. They were looking for a father for themselves.

The realization was like a fist around her heart. There was nothing she could do, nothing she could say, to make that situation any different. She'd stayed in one marriage, thinking it best for her children, but they'd been hurt anyway. She had no intention of making a mistake like that ever again.

"Of course you can go on the camping trip," she said, wrapping her arms around her sons and pulling them close to her. They squirmed against her, then broke into giggles when she started to tickle them.

"So it's okay, then?" Breathless, still laughing, Cody rolled away. "About the ad?"

Oh, yes. The ad. Still kneeling beside the bed, she groaned and fell face forward on Cody's bed.

What was she going to do now? Call the paper, of course, except it was too late now. She'd have to call first thing in the morning. But all those issues already out there, and all those calls on her machine...

"Tell you what," she said with a sigh, "next time you boys want to surprise me, let me know first, okay?"

Cody screwed up his face. "That's silly, Mom. It wouldn't be a surprise then, would it?"

Exactly what she didn't need any more of. She thought of Slater downstairs. Perhaps that was the one good thing that had come out of this. It felt good to know that he cared enough to come check up on her because he thought she was in trouble. She'd simply go downstairs and explain everything.

And then he would leave.

She felt a dull ache deep inside her, but dismissed it. So he'd leave. What did she expect? Of course he'd leave. He had a life, she had a life. Tonight they'd catch up on old news, then he'd be on his way. She'd go on with her life, and so would he.

By the time she reached the bottom of the stairs, she still hadn't a clue what to say. She drew in a long breath, then headed for the kitchen. She'd just tell him. They'd have a good laugh, he'd stay for dinner, he'd leave and that would be the end of it.

He was pacing from the back door to the kitchen sink when she walked into the kitchen, his frown dark and impatient.

"Slater—"

He stalked over to her. "Kasey, sit down."

"Slater, I know how this—"

"Sit." He pointed to the kitchen chair.

Kasey frowned. Hadn't she just gone through this with her kids, only in reverse? She most certainly wasn't a child anymore, even if he thought she was.

But children had taught her patience, she reasoned. And Slater seemed so determined to have his say, and ignore hers, why not let him go on for a while? Folding her arms, she sat in the chair and looked up at him.

He dragged both hands through his thick hair. "Kase, you're obviously in some kind of trouble. It's understandable how hard life must be for you. Raising two kids by yourself, no husband and all."

Exactly the way she wanted it.

"But placing an ad like that, Kase, it's dangerous, and I just have to say, downright foolish. God only knows who might try to take advantage of your vulnerability."

Foolish? Vulnerable? She pressed her lips tightly together, hoping that Mr. Hugh Slater was hungry, because she was about to serve him a big helping of crow.

"Slater, I know how this looks, but that ad was placed with the best of intentions and—"

"The best of intentions!" Hands on his hips, he stood over her. "It's just plain stupid."

She felt suddenly defensive of her sons. What they'd done, they'd done out of love. They wanted her to be happy. There was *nothing* stupid about that. She rose slowly and leveled her gaze with his. "Stupid?"

His voice gentled as he took hold of her shoulders. "Look, I'm sorry. In my entire life, I've never stuck my nose in anyone's business. But this is different. This is you, Kasey. We go way back, no matter how many years in between. When I saw that ad, my gut told me I had to stop you. You have every right to be mad at me, for leaving like I did ten years ago. All I'm asking now is that you don't do anything rash. That you'll think about this."

His words, his hands on her shoulders, made it difficult to think at all. Suddenly ten years, and all that had happened in between, melted away…

She sat in the church pew. Her mother wept quietly beside her, while her father dabbed at his own moisture-filled eyes. On her left, Slater sat rigid, his face pale. And to Slater's left, Jack Slater stared ahead, unblinking, emotionless, as the service began.

"Death is never easy." Reverend Green looked out at the crowded pews, his face grim, his voice solemn. "But the death of one so young, with such promise, is beyond words."

Kasey had told herself she'd be strong. That Jeanie would have wanted her to be. But the blackness inside her, the emptiness, kept pulling at her, threatening to overtake her. She kept her eyes to the front of the church, at the flowers covering the casket.

It wasn't Jeanie. It wasn't.

An arm came around her shoulders. Slater. When had she started to cry? He pulled her close, held her. She would have crawled inside him if she could. It would be safe there.

She knew he was leaving. He hadn't told her, but she'd seen his bags in the back of his truck.

"Slater," she whispered. "Take me with you."

He stilled, but said nothing.

"Please don't leave me, too," she murmured. "I love you."

She felt, more than heard, his sigh. He cradled her against him, ran his hand over her hair. She breathed in the scent of his aftershave, felt the strong, steady beat of his heart under her fingertips, and she knew she'd never love again...

"Kasey, are you listening to me? I want you to think about this, that's all I'm asking."

Blinking slowly, she stared at Slater, forcing herself to focus on his words. How young and foolish she'd been. Of course she'd loved again. She'd met Paul one year later, hadn't she?

She stepped away from Slater's touch, from the heat that had begun to swirl up her spine. "I appreciate your concern, but there's nothing to think about."

"Kasey—" He turned and threw his hands out with exasperation. "You can't just marry some strange guy. Let's talk about this. Whatever problems you might—"

"There's nothing to talk about. I'm not marrying a strange guy. I'm not marrying anyone."

He hesitated, then slowly turned back toward her. "You aren't?"

"No. I never was."

"You weren't?"

She shook her head.

"But the ad, with your name and the Double D..."

Patience touched her smile. "I'm afraid my boys are the culprits. When we were in Dallas I placed an ad for a stud—as in stallion—for the mare I just bought. Cody and Troy decided to surprise me with an ad of their own."

Kasey's sons placed the ad? Slater suddenly found that he couldn't speak. Perhaps it was due to the fact that his foot was in his mouth. He sank slowly into a chair at the kitchen table and simply stared at her.

She sat across from him, then flipped her hair off her shoulders and laughed hesitantly. "Somewhere they got the crazy idea that I, uh, could use a husband."

Her cheeks flushed bright pink, emphasizing the deep green of her eyes. He felt like an idiot, talking to her as he had. Ten years might have made him older, but it sure as hell hadn't made him any smarter.

"And here I thought I was saving you from doing something foolish," he said, shaking his head. "Too bad there wasn't someone to save me."

"I'm glad there wasn't," she said quietly, holding her gaze steady with his. "Ten years is too long."

The look in her eyes warmed him. It felt good, sitting in the kitchen with Kasey. He'd spent many an hour here, with the Donovans, at this very table, eating, talking, laughing.

He covered her hand with his and linked fingers. "I'm sorry about your folks, Kase. I was out of the country when it happened. By the time I found out and called, the number was disconnected. I didn't know how to reach you."

There was a high-pitched squeal from upstairs, a stomping of feet and the slam of a door. Kasey seemed oblivious to it.

"Paul and I never stayed in one place very long. The

seven years we were married, I think we moved five times. He was easily bored.''

There was something in Kasey's voice and the upward lift of her chin that had Slater's jaw tightening and his protective defenses kicking into overdrive. He knew enough about pride to understand he couldn't ask her about it. Not yet, anyway. "And the past two years?"

"The boys and I stayed in New York. I had a great job with an investment company that paid for schooling and offered flexible hours for working mothers. It gave me a chance to spend more time with my sons, take the classes I needed for my degree, and make a few good investments.'' The ceiling fan over the kitchen table shook from a sudden pounding overhead. Kasey ignored it. "I'd had the ranch leased out, and once I had enough money saved, I came back here. I'm boarding a few horses right now, and as soon as I find the right stud for Miss Lucy, I'm going to start raising quarter horses. My boys are going to have the kind of life they deserve.''

Determination shone in her eyes. A fierce love for her children that summoned an unexpected stab of envy in his gut. Thank God there were mothers like Kasey to make up for the Paul Morgans and Jack Slaters in the world.

"Listen,'' she whispered suddenly.

He did, but there was only quiet. Confused, he watched her straighten in her chair, her green eyes narrowing. She pulled her hand from his, and he couldn't help but notice how smooth and soft her fingers were against his calloused palms. He started to say something, but she put one long, tapered finger to her lips. Lips that were wide and turned up at the corners, lips that could make a man forget himself.

Which was exactly what he was doing, dammit. He

gave himself a mental kick and reined in his unwanted thoughts. "I don't hear anything."

"Exactly. And therein lies the problem. Prepare yourself, Slater."

"Prepare myself for—"

They hit with all the vengeance of a tornado. Two screaming banshees blew into the kitchen, arms flailing and feet flying. Troy was in the lead, his shrieks a mixture of terror and laughter; Cody was on his brother's heels, his red face blazing with anger, his hair wet and dripping with green goo.

"I'm gonna rip your liver out," Cody wailed. Troy stuck out his tongue. Slater ducked as Cody flung a wad of the green slime at Troy. They circled the table twice, then darted out the back door.

Slater stared at the open back door. "Shouldn't we be calling the paramedics?"

Kasey's laugh was deeper than he'd remembered, richer. "You haven't been around kids much, have you?"

Hardly. Jared Stone had a two-month-old baby, and Jake, Jared's brother, had a one-month-old. At a family gathering only a few days ago, Savannah, Jake's wife, had insisted that Slater hold both babies for a picture. Before he knew it, he'd been corralled onto the couch with a tiny baby girl in each arm. He'd faced guerrillas in South America and wild bulls in Texas that hadn't terrified him half as much. "Can't say that I have."

"Well, Slater," she said with a sigh, "you're about to get an education. You might as well sit back and relax."

The front door banged open.

"Stupid face!"

"Dog breath!"

"Wussy!"

"Dork!"

They blasted up the stairs in a salvo of insults. The air seemed to quiver in their wake.

Kasey frowned, then rose. The firm set of her mouth and the hard look in her eyes had Slater feeling sorry for the boys. It also had him glad he wasn't the subject of whatever sentence was about to be laid down.

"I'll make up the guest room after I 'speak' to my sons. You're staying the night."

He opened his mouth to decline, then shut it again when he saw the firm set of her mouth. He folded his hands in his lap and nodded. "Yes, ma'am."

She grinned, then stopped at the kitchen door and looked at him. "By the way, Slate, you might want to wash that green slime off the back of your head before it dries."

Three

Slater rose early, even before the sun began to push its first rays across the horizon. He pulled on a navy T-shirt, worn jeans and boots, then quietly made his way down the stairs.

Dinner had been quite an experience last night, he remembered with a smile. A noisy one. Excited from their trip, Cody and Troy had talked at the same time, relating every detail of their vacation. Kasey continually reminded them of their manners, corrected their grammar and pushed the green beans. While they were clearing the table, both boys insisted they weren't even a little tired and couldn't they stay up and watch "Hannibal's Heroes"? How else would they find out who had stolen Yuma Blackhawk's telepathic crystal ring?

Kasey sent them upstairs for baths, but before the coffee had finished brewing, both boys were sprawled, half dressed, out cold on their beds. They obviously slept as hard as they played, Slater had thought as he'd stood at the bedroom door and watched Kasey kiss her sons goodnight. His own mother had died before he'd even turned ten, but he remembered her whispered "sleep tight," as she'd tuck him in every night, and the memory had brought a tightening in his chest.

He closed the back door behind him with a soft click, careful not to let the screen door slam. He knew that Kasey needed the sleep as much as her boys. They'd stayed up and talked until long after midnight, covering the highlights of each other's life for the past ten years, but the long drive from Dallas had taken its toll on her and he'd sent her to bed mimicking the same parental tone she'd used on her sons. She'd gone under protest, and only after he'd promised to fill her in on every juicy detail of his life in the morning.

The air was crisp this morning, the inside of the barn pungent with the scent of horse and leather and alfalfa. He heard a soft whinny, then a rustling of hay as the animals stirred. So familiar, he thought. Every smell, every sound a reminder of another time, another place.

A place he'd sworn never to come back to.

With a sigh, he picked up a rake. The wood felt solid and smooth under his hand. He hadn't mucked out a stall in ten years, but the rhythm came back easily to him. So did pitching hay, he found, after he'd cleaned six occupied stalls. Effortlessly, he swung the pitchfork into the bale, hooked a bite, then arched the flake over his shoulder into the stall of a pretty little chestnut mare. She munched daintily, then blew out a delicate snort of thanks.

"You're welcome," Slater mumbled, and stabbed the fork back into the bale. His next customer, an unusually fine-looking speckled gray, nodded his approval, then turned his attention to his breakfast.

Slater had been working in near darkness, but now the dawn light began to spill into the barn through the open doors. And, he noted with a frown, through the roof, as well.

Leaning against the pitchfork, Slater surveyed the interior of the barn. It was neat and clean, but in desperate need of repairs. Holes in the roof, missing doors on the three end stalls, rotting wood. Only the stalls that housed the horses had been rebuilt.

He'd noticed the inside of Kasey's house had shown signs of wear also. The kitchen faucet had rattled and leaked, the screens in the spare bedroom and upstairs bathroom were torn, a window in the living room cracked and the front porch steps ready to cave in.

Maybe her kids weren't so far off after all, Slater thought. Maybe she could use a husband.

He shook his head at the ridiculous idea and tossed a flake of hay to a sorrel gelding in the next stall. Of course Kasey didn't need a husband. A leaky faucet and broken window hardly required matrimony.

"Hugh Slater, what exactly do you think you're doing?"

Pitchfork in hand, he swung around. She stood at the barn's entrance, hands on her denim-clad hips, frowning at him. He swiped at the sweat beaded on his brow, then stabbed the pitchfork into the mound of hay and rested his hands on top of the handle. "Good morning."

She folded her arms, then tossed her head to shake back the auburn curls spilling over the shoulders of her slate blue blouse. "Don't 'good morning' me, mister. You're supposed to be in bed, not mucking out stalls and feeding horses."

There was purpose in her stride as she marched toward him, and it was impossible not to notice the sway of her slender hips. Curves had definitely settled in all the right places on her. If the lady was looking for a husband, or anything else, there would no doubt be a long line of males eager to oblige.

"Man's got to pay for his room and board somehow," he said, holding tight when she covered his hands with hers and tried to tug the pitchfork away. "Besides, I wanted to see if I still had the touch."

She smiled at him. "Slater, you always had the touch, don't you know that?"

She'd said the words innocently enough, but an undercurrent moved between them, an unspoken hint of something that had his hands tightening on the pitchfork handle.

Her fingers were warm and smooth over his, her skin soft. Before he could stop the thought, he wondered if she was that soft all over.

A mare from the fourth stall whinnied loudly, complaining she hadn't been fed. Slater nodded toward the distressed animal, thankful for the interruption, uneasy with his reaction to Kasey's touch. "At least let me finish what I started. Then I promise I'll sit on my butt and do nothing."

And a nice butt it is, Kasey noted as he turned away, then had to swallow back a gasp at her unexpected thought. Something had just passed between them a moment ago, something that still had her a little shaken, yet a little exhilarated at the same time. What would have happened, she wondered, if they'd have let themselves explore the awareness that had sparked between them, if they'd leaned closer and crossed over the invisible line that had been drawn between them?

Chastising herself for such an outrageous thought, a thought that had no possible chance of becoming a reality, Kasey scooped up a bucket of oats and moved down the row of stalls, following behind Slater, watching him feed the horses as she had hundreds of times before at his father's ranch.

He'd carefully avoided any discussion of his father last night. They'd talked about jobs they'd had, people they'd both known, who'd gotten married or moved, but if the conversation even came close to mentioning his father, then Slater immediately changed the subject.

It wasn't easy to discuss what was happening in Granite Ridge and avoid the name of Jack Slater and the Bar S. The man and the ranch were icons in Granite Ridge and the surrounding counties. He was known as far north as Amarillo and as far south as San Antonio as one of the wealthiest and finest breeders of quarter horses. He was also known as an overbearing, hard businessman who demanded perfection. Which would have also described him as a father.

"So what do you think of my boarders?" She ran her hand over the chestnut mare's velvety nose.

"Nice stock." He tossed the last fleck of hay into the end stall. "Especially the gray and the chestnut you're petting. They look young, but they've got strong cutting potential. The others are good for riding, except for that little sorrel on the end. She's a tad high-strung, though nothing a little work and a few sweet words wouldn't fix."

He was right. But that didn't surprise her. Ten years ago, Slater had been the best horseman around. He could make the most difficult bronc do wheelies, then beg to pull a plow. "I hope to have a full stable by the end of the year. With that income and Miss Lucy as a brood-mare, the Double D will be good as new in no time.''

''Ah, yes, Miss Lucy.'' He stabbed the pitchfork into a bale of hay and grinned. ''The blushing bride. When are you expecting her?''

''Tomorrow.'' She tossed a handful of oats to the gray and glanced over her shoulder at Slater. ''I wish you could see her.''

It was an unspoken invitation to stay. They both knew it. Slater's dark gaze met hers and the awkward silence hovered between them.

''I have to get going, Kase,'' he said finally.

Dammit, dammit, dammit. Why had she let herself get her hopes up, even for a second? She'd known from the moment she laid eyes on him that he'd had no intention of staying. Ten years may have passed, but nothing had really changed. Not his feelings for Granite Ridge and his father.

Not his feelings for her. She was still his kid sister's best friend, nothing more.

She swung the bucket of oats to the next stall, forcing a lightness to her voice that contradicted the heaviness in her heart. ''What about all those juicy tidbits of your life you promised?''

He gave her a cocky smile. ''Yeah, well that should take all of about five minutes.''

She doubted that. There was a look in his eyes, something in the way he carried himself and the tone of his voice that told her there was much more than he'd ever let on. And last night, even though they'd talked half the night, she still knew nothing significant about the past ten years. Everything he'd told her had been superficial and decidedly vague.

''I'm going in to town to straighten things out at the

newspaper.'' She brushed her hands off on her jeans.
''We could have breakfast at Callie's. She still makes the
best blueberry waffles in the county.''

''And the best corn muffins.'' His expression was one
of reverence, then he slowly shook his head. ''It's better
this way, Kase.''

She couldn't help the knot of anger tightening in her
chest. Mission accomplished. There were no maidens to
rescue, so it was ''*Hasta la vista,* baby.''

''Will you say goodbye to the boys?''

''I wasn't just going to drive off,'' he said with a
frown. ''Are they up yet?''

As if on cue, they came charging into the barn, whoop-
ing like wild beasts wearing baseball caps and blue jeans.
Cody had a glove and ball, Troy a baseball bat. ''Hey,
Slater,'' Troy called, ''wanna hit a few?''

''Slater has to leave now,'' Kasey said, amazed that
she was able to keep her voice even. ''Come say goodbye
and thank him for helping with your chores.''

Troy bumped into the back of Cody when he stopped
suddenly. ''Leaving. You mean, like really leaving, not
coming back?'' Cody asked.

Kasey started to answer, then thought better of it. He
hadn't made it easy for her ten years ago when he'd left,
had he? Why should she make it easy for him now?

Slater looked at her, then glanced back at the boys and
cleared his throat. ''I was just stopping by to say hi to
your mom,'' he mumbled awkwardly. ''I'm glad I got to
meet you, though.''

They stared up at him for a long moment, then Troy
said, ''Where you going?''

''Uh, Alaska.''

''Where's Alaska?'' Troy asked.

"It's far away," Cody answered with authority. "And it's real cold."

Kasey smiled knowingly at Slater. He frowned at her, then knelt in front of the boys so he could look them in the eye. "Alaska is a beautiful place. You should go there sometime with your mom."

Troy shook his head. "I like it here. It's not cold, either. We don't have to stay inside all the time."

Confinement had always been difficult for her sons, Kasey thought. They hated being inside, and had disliked the heavy clothing and jackets, as well. "We need to go into town now, boys. Say goodbye to Slater."

"'Bye." There was no enthusiasm in Cody's voice as he tossed the baseball back and forth between his hand and glove.

"'Bye." Troy stepped closer to Cody, dragging the bat on the ground.

"Take care," Slater said with a smile, then stood.

Kasey tried to swallow the lump that had settled in her throat, but it refused to budge. No matter how much she wanted him to stay, she wouldn't ask, and she sure as hell wasn't going to cry.

"It was good to see you, Slate," she said. "Stop by again sometime in the next millennium. If I'm lucky, I'll have grandkids."

"I'm sorry, Kasey." He reached out and tugged her into his arms. "I wish it could be different."

She leaned against him, breathed in the smell of him, a mixture of man and horse and hay. It would have to last her a long time. Most likely a lifetime.

"Would you like me to tell your father anything?" She had to try one last time, as a parent, as Slater's friend.

"No." He dropped his arms away. "I'll give you a call. Drop a postcard."

She nodded, but they both knew he wouldn't. She also knew she didn't want to watch him drive away again. "I want to be at the newspaper when they open. You're welcome to use the shower and help yourself to breakfast. There's muffins and apples on the counter in the kitchen."

His smile never reached his eyes. "Take care of yourself, Kase."

"I always have, Slate," she said, then turned and walked away with her sons.

Slater had already showered, stuffed his dirty clothes into his duffel bag and was headed out the back door when the phone rang. He hesitated, knowing she hadn't cleared her answering machine and it couldn't pick up any more messages. He also knew how important it was to her to find that stud for Miss Lucy.

He picked it up on the third ring. "Double D."

"Kasey there?" a man asked.

"Not right now." He spotted a bowl of apples on the counter and reached for a big red one. "Can I help you?"

"I'm calling about her ad." He coughed deeply. A smoker's cough, Slater noted. "Tell the little lady she need look no farther. Jimmy Webster from the Circle J is on his way."

Jimmy Webster spoke with a rhyming twang that set Slater's teeth on edge. "Is this about—"

"Tell her I'll be there by eight. We can do a little test run."

Slater narrowed his eyes. "Test run?"

"Sure, man. No one signs on the dotted line without a little sample. You understand."

Slater was beginning to understand only too well. This was definitely not a call about a horse.

Something evil came over him. His hand tightened around the phone in his hand and he stared hard at the apple he was quickly turning into applesauce.

"Kasey should be back in a couple of hours, Jimmy," he said casually. "He, I mean, *she,* damn, I still get confused since the operation. Anyway, *she* should be back from the barbershop, I mean, hair salon, real soon. I can have, uh, *her* call you in a little while."

Silence echoed from the receiver, then a click and the dial tone hummed loudly.

Grinning, Slater bit into the softened apple and hung up the phone. Mr. Jimmy Webster wouldn't come within ten miles of the Double D now. That jerk could take a test drive right off the edge of a steep cliff. He chewed thoughtfully, staring at the messages on the machine. Undoubtably there were several more of the same kinds of calls. There was no telling how many weirdos and perverts might show up at her door.

Some other idiot just might want to take a little test drive, too, he thought with a frown. Just pulling the ad Cody and Troy had placed wouldn't get rid of all the other morons who'd think that Kasey would be an easy target.

And the thought of even one of those clowns coming near Kasey or her sons made his blood boil.

He finished off the apple in four more bites and tossed the core into the trash. She could use some help around the place, though. Someone handy, with some ranching experience. Someone with a little free time on his hands.

Someone like him.

No, he thought, tugging his hat low on his head. He'd only come here to talk to her. He was no white knight. Kasey would be fine. She was a big girl now. A woman, he corrected.

Most definitely, a woman.

He turned on the faucet to rinse his hands. It sputtered and groaned, then spewed out an erratic stream of hot water, though he'd turned on the cold.

Muttering an oath, he snapped the water off and headed for his truck.

"Mom, how come Mr. Plucket yells when he talks?"

Kasey had already turned off Main Street and was heading back to the ranch. She resisted the urge to honk at Mrs. Gardner's slow-moving station wagon on the open road in front of her. It wasn't the elderly woman's problem that Kasey was in a bad mood and was consumed with an overwhelming need to drive faster than twenty miles an hour.

"Mr. Plucket wasn't wearing his hearing aid, honey. Since he can't hear, he thinks that no one else can, either."

Kasey had explained to the newspaper editor that the ad for a husband was a big mistake. In fact, she'd explained three times, very loudly, that she wanted the ad removed immediately. He'd pulled up her file, grinned at her and the boys, then nodded he'd take care of it right away.

It had not been a good morning. Sandra Winters from the drugstore had said good-morning to her outside the *Granite Ridge Gazette* office, and Kasey was certain she'd heard a giggle after they'd passed. And Darren Brown at the gas station had looked at her, too. A long, hard, sweeping glance, as if he was considering a lot more than pumping her gas.

She didn't like the look one little bit.

Maybe she should have taken another ad out, she thought irritably.

Notice: Kasey Donovan Morgan is not looking for a husband. She is happy single and intends to stay that way.

Mrs. Gardner finally pulled off the highway into her own driveway, waving as Kasey drove by. She felt guilty that she'd been annoyed with the woman's speed. That was one of the reasons Kasey had wanted to come back here and raise her sons: everyone took their time here, watched out for their neighbor.

But Mrs. Gardner's driving wasn't the reason Kasey was out of sorts, she realized as she pulled into the driveway leading to the ranch. Nor was it the ad her sons had placed or what anyone in town thought.

It was Slater.

He'd be gone by now, of course. She stopped the truck in front of her house. Cody and Troy bounced out of the cab and bounded up the front steps. Less than twenty-four hours ago he'd been standing right there, on her porch. Now he was on his way to Alaska. She'd been nothing more than a slight delay in his plans. His good deed for the decade.

It made her mad as hell. It made her absolutely furious. It made her—

She rested her forehead on the steering wheel and sighed. It made her miserable.

And that made her even madder.

Slamming the car door behind her, she straightened her shoulders and strode purposefully into the house. As unpleasant a task as it was going to be, she needed to deal with all those phone calls and the mail her sons' ad had inspired. She'd put it off last night because of Slater, but she knew she couldn't rest until she'd answered every prospective groom and informed them the wedding was off. She also had to sort out any responses for the stud and answer those calls and letters, as well.

She closed the front door behind her, tossing her purse on the entry stand as she rubbed at the pounding ache over her left eye. The horses needed to be exercised, she had to get a stall ready for Miss Lucy, there were piles of laundry from their trip and somewhere under the weeds in her garden she might find a ripe tomato or green bean.

Kasey followed the sound of her sons' voices in the kitchen. She'd let them each have a donut from the convenience market at the gas station, but that was at least thirty minutes ago and no doubt they were raiding the refrigerator.

They were standing at the kitchen sink when she walked in. Still massaging the pain over her eye, Kasey headed for the pantry. "Tuna fish today, boys," she said, preparing herself for an argument. "A handful of corn chips and an apple. That's the menu and I'm not in the mood for any complaints."

"Sounds good to me."

At the sound of the deep, familiar voice, Kasey froze. She turned slowly, fingers still pressed to her temple.

Slater?

She heard him. She just didn't *see* him. All she saw was Cody and Troy, standing at the sink, looking down. The kitchen table in the middle of the floor hid from her what they were looking at.

She moved around the table and there he was. Or at least, there was *half* of him. She stared at the long, denim-enclosed legs protruding from under her sink. The toes of his black cowboy boots pointed to the ceiling; grease smudged his thighs. When her gaze moved upward, just below his waist, and lingered a little too long, she quickly snapped her attention to the pipe Slater had a stranglehold on.

"What in the world are you doing?" she asked calmly, though her pulse was skipping.

"Slater's fixing the pipe." A grin split Cody's face. "It's rusty and he's going to wash it."

"Not wash it," Slater corrected. "I replaced the washers in the faucet and a section of the drainpipe. Boys, hand me that wrench by your mother's foot, will you?"

Four little hands grabbed the tool and handed it under the sink. If there'd have been room, they'd have climbed in alongside him.

He was supposed to be gone, dammit. She sat back on her heels and watched him wrestle the corroded pipes. She'd already settled her emotions into neat little corners. Now they were spinning again.

And she was going to have to say goodbye all over again this afternoon.

"Slater." She reached in and took hold of the wrench. "*What* are you doing here?"

He lifted his head, bumped his forehead on the pipes and bit back a curse. Kasey hadn't the slightest sympathy.

"There was water everywhere, Kase," he said, rubbing at his head. "All over the floor, under the sink. I couldn't just leave it like that."

She looked around the hardwood kitchen floor. Dry as a bone. With the same rim of dust along the baseboard that had settled in during her vacation. She narrowed her eyes at him. "All over the floor?"

"Okay, well maybe just some water under the sink," he said with a shrug, and tugged the wrench away from her. "But it would have been all over if I hadn't caught it in time. It's a good thing I carry tools in my truck, and I remembered where your dad kept his plumbing supplies in the garage. Do you put big chunks of celery in your tuna like your mom used to?''

"Yes, I do. Slater, I don't want you doing this. I was going to call a plumber." When it broke, she thought, knowing she wouldn't have spent the money until it was absolutely necessary. A little clanking in the pipes and a few drops of water under the sink were hardly grounds for calling a plumber.

"Well, now you don't have to. I've almost got this disassembled and after I replace the rusted pipe it'll be good as new. Can I have my bread toasted?''

Lord help her, she thought, not knowing whether to laugh or strangle the man. She rose with a sigh and gathered the makings for sandwiches while Cody and Troy knelt beside Slater, watching him work and listening intently while Slater explained what he was doing.

Paul had never had that kind of attention for his sons. When he was home, which wasn't often, he was working. He'd never once replaced a washer or even changed a lightbulb, let alone taken the time to explain anything mechanical.

She'd just finished mixing the tuna and was putting the bread into the toaster when the phone rang. It was George Murdock, the man she'd bought Miss Lucy from. They firmed up the delivery of the horse and she was off the phone again as the toast popped up.

"That was Mr. Murdock," she told her sons while she heaped the sandwiches with tuna and lettuce. She knew Cody and Troy would pull out the lettuce, but she could only hope they might ingest an accidental bite. "He hurt his back and can't deliver Miss Lucy until Friday.''

"That's forever," Cody complained. "We wanted Slater to see her.''

She fought back the sudden twist in her stomach and

set four glasses on the table. "It's only three days, and Slater's on his way to Alaska, remember?"

"You can stay, can't you?" Troy asked quietly. "Just to see Miss Lucy?"

"Yeah, Slater." Cody shook Slater's leg. "It's only three days."

The twist in Kasey's stomach turned into a knot. "Boys, Alaska is a long way—"

"Sure. I can stay," Slater said around a grunt.

Kasey was glad she'd already set the glasses down. Otherwise she'd be picking glass up off the floor. *I can stay?* Why had he changed his mind so suddenly?

She looked at him, watched his arms flex and ripple as he strained at the rusted pipe. That roller coaster at the amusement park did less to her equilibrium than Hugh Slater.

"If your mom says it's okay," Slater added, his voice and arms shaking from the force he exerted on the pipe. "Stand back, boys."

They jumped out of the way just in time. The pipe let loose and flew out from under the sink. It ricocheted off a kitchen chair, then skidded across the floor and landed at Kasey's feet. Both boys cheered and clapped. Slater waved the wrench in a victory salute.

Kasey stood there, staring down at the still spinning pipe, afraid that her heart was about to follow the same path.

"Sure he can stay," she said, feeling dazed. Absently, she gathered up the sandwiches and put them on the table. "Now wash up for lunch."

Between heartbeats she realized what she'd said, but she wasn't fast enough. She heard the sound of running water, then a loud, animal-like roar.

Her mouth dropped open as she watched Slater unfold

his long body from under the sink. His hair was flattened to his head, his T-shirt drenched.

She tried to stop herself, truly she did, but it was no use. Holding her sides, she sank to the floor and laughed her head off.

Four

Kasey had no idea there were so many men looking for a wife.

She sat at the kitchen table, staring at the mound of mail from prospective husbands. She'd known that the *Gazette* reached all the local counties and neighboring towns, but she'd never realized so many people actually read the personals, let alone answered ads of that nature. She'd managed to answer nearly half the responses she'd brought home two days ago, but, to her frustration, the mail kept coming.

And the phone messages. A shiver wiggled up her spine as she remembered listening to all the calls on her answering machine. Just hearing some of their voices, not to mention a couple of rather crude messages, brought forth another shiver.

She'd explained five times in the past forty-eight hours that the ad was a mistake, she wasn't looking for a husband, and no, thank you, she didn't want to "go out on a date and get to know each other a little better."

And to top it all off, when she'd opened her Thursday edition of the *Gazette* this morning, she found out that Mr. Plucket had pulled the ad for the stud service and left the ad for a husband. She'd had to drive back into town today and had shouted at the hard-of-hearing editor to make certain he understood her this time. Now, looking at all this mail, she felt like screaming, but she simply didn't have the voice left, or the energy.

And then there was Slater.

She folded her arms on the tabletop and rested her chin on top. She smiled at the image of his dripping hair and soaked T-shirt when he'd emerged sputtering from under the open pipe yesterday. Cody and Troy had run and hid behind her, not quite sure what an angry six-foot-five, soaking wet man might do. He'd come at them, his grin sinister, snatched one under each arm, then took them outside and sprayed them with the hose. They'd screamed and laughed until they were all soaking wet and full of mud. She'd made them all eat outside, cleaned up the kitchen floor, then had her sons strip at the back door and come in to shower. She'd considered making Slater strip, as well, but he'd escaped by hosing the mud off and changing into dry clothes in the barn.

Much to her disappointment.

She sighed and closed her eyes. She was thinking way too much about him. About that single shock of dark brown hair that continually fell over his right eye. The way his jeans fit low on his lean hips. That little wicked half smile that lit his dark eyes whenever he was about to roughhouse with her sons.

Cody and Troy followed him around like puppy dogs. And though she'd repeatedly told Slater not to, every time she turned around he was fixing something: a leaky faucet, the broken sprinkler on the side of the house, her squeaky oven door. If she turned her back for more than five minutes, he had either a wrench or screwdriver in his hand. No matter what time she set her alarm for, he was up before her and out feeding the horses.

Which reminded her. When she'd put the boys down for bed he'd gone out to the barn to "turn off a light." Or so he'd told her. That was nearly a half hour ago. He was probably digging her a new well, or painting the barn. She was beginning to think he kept himself busy fixing things just so he wouldn't have to sit and talk with her.

Well, enough of that, she thought, standing up and heading for the back door. What did he stay for, if he was avoiding her at every turn? She knew perfectly well he hadn't stayed to see Miss Lucy, so there was obviously something else on his mind. If she had to hog tie the man to make him start talking, then so be it.

Autumn touched the night air. A breeze rippled through the sycamores behind the house and sent leaves scurrying over the ground. The scent of wild roses drifted from the vines climbing up the trellis over the back porch. The owl living in her barn perched somewhere in a tall maple beside the corrals and softly hooted his evening song.

Kasey stuck her hands into her back jeans' pockets and slowed her pace, breathing it all in. This was all hers now. Hers and Cody's and Troy's. She knew her parents would be happy their grandchildren were here, and the thought made her smile.

The light was still on in the barn, but there was no sign of Slater. She started to call out, then heard the rustle of hay in the stall she'd designated for Miss Lucy. Kasey had planned on replacing the rotted wood in the stall tomorrow and cleaning it out. She'd specifically told Slater it was off-limits, but he hadn't listened to her before, so why now?

She moved to the stall, expecting to find him with nails in his teeth and a hammer in his hand. Instead, he knelt in the corner, rolling a quarter over and under the fingers of one hand. Back and forth, back and forth, as if in a trance.

"Slater?"

Startled, he dropped the coin in the thick hay and looked up at her. He smiled, but not before she saw the pain shadowed in his eyes. "Hey, Kase."

"Hey, yourself." She sank down on her knees and searched through the hay for the quarter she'd made him drop. "Sorry if I surprised you."

Slater chuckled, watching Kasey rummage through the hay, thinking what an understatement that was. She'd surprised him, all right. From the moment she'd opened her front door and he'd stepped into her life. "Finish answering your fan mail?"

Groaning, she tossed her head back. Her neck was long and smooth, he noted. Her auburn hair shimmered red and gold under the dim barn light and tumbled loose over her shoulders and down her back. "I've decided it would be easier to move and change my name. What do you think of Clementine Hoodwinker?"

Because he needed something to do rather than stare at Kasey, he began to root through the hay, also. "Nah. You look more like a Henrietta or an Enid."

"Enid?" She wrinkled her nose. "Thanks. I'll pick my own name. I got enough teasing in my life over Acacia."

"Not from me you didn't. I always liked your name."

She laughed, and the sound was like a ripple of silk

over his skin. He sifted through hay, searching for that damn quarter as if it were a parachute and his plane was going down.

"You were the only one who ever called me Acacia without making fun or reprimanding. Ta-dah!" Smiling, she held up the quarter.

With a grin, Slater took the coin, then opened his hand. It was gone. She frowned, but there was admiration in her green eyes. "Now, you want to tell me what you're doing out here, besides practicing magic tricks?"

"It beats smoking," he said, wishing he had a cigarette right now, though he'd quit them eight years ago. She held her gaze steady with his, waiting for a real answer.

He sighed, then twisted his body and pulled out a rotted piece of wood at the back of the stall, exposing a hole. "Come here."

She moved closer and peered inside the opening in the stall, but she saw only darkness. "What?"

"Look closer."

Squinting, she practically put her nose in the hole. Something moved. She jumped back, but Slater held her arm and laughed softly. "They won't hurt you."

"Said the spider to the fly," she said with a shiver.

"No spiders, no snakes. Just look."

Her look was skeptical, but she took a deep breath and leaned back to stare into the hole.

"Oh, Slater," she whispered after a moment. "They're so tiny and sweet."

He smiled. "Well, I wouldn't exactly call baby mice sweet, but they are tiny. They can't be more than a few days' old. I was going to replace all this old wood when I found the nest."

She cocked her head and frowned at him. "I thought

I told you——'' She sighed with exasperation and shook her head. ''Never mind. Just tell me where you were.''

''Where I was?''

''When I came in here a minute ago.'' She leaned back against the stall and leveled her gaze with his. ''You were in a galaxy far, far away. Can we talk about it?''

He pulled out the quarter and made it dance over his knuckles. ''Talk about what?''

She covered his hand with hers. ''You know what.''

He hadn't noticed the scar on her thumb before. A tiny jagged line just under the knuckle. He touched it lightly with the tip of his finger.

''I think Jeanie was about nine when she found them behind a box of old magazines in the shed,'' he said after a long moment. ''Baby raccoons. There were three of them, with little miniature masks around shiny black eyes. She dragged me out there to see them the minute I came home from football practice. She'd already named them Teddy, Freddy and Eddy.''

He smiled and leaned back against the stall beside Kasey. ''Like any nine-year-old, she wanted to keep them. I told her that they had a mother and she shouldn't touch them, and she said, what if they didn't have a mother? What if their mother had died, like ours had, and they had no one to take care of them? I told her they still had a daddy and they'd be fine.''

''I remember,'' Kasey said, smiling. ''She was so excited she called me that night. We went to the shed the next day, but they weren't there. She said the mother must have moved them.''

One of the horses stamped a foot and whinnied softly; in the distance an owl hooted. Slater had forgotten how peaceful it was here, how time seemed to stroll rather than race. He pulled his hand from hers and skipped the quarter over his knuckles again. "The mother didn't move them. My father heard her call you and killed them all the next morning. Said they'd just eat the grain."

Kasey closed her eyes and drew in a slow, steadying breath. "She never told me."

"She wouldn't have wanted to upset you. Besides, that's how we dealt with problems in my house—ignore them, pretend they didn't exist." He closed his fist tightly around the quarter and stared blankly at his hand. When he opened it again, the coin was gone. "How could I have known that warm family trait would be her death warrant?"

Guilt and grief were cruel taskmasters, Kasey thought sadly. Slater had warred with those demons for ten years. She saw it in the sharp edge of his dark eyes. "You weren't driving the car, Slater," Kasey said softly.

Slater's jaw tightened. "If she'd come to me before she left with that son of a bitch, she wouldn't have been in that car at all."

Glen Wilson had always been bad news, Kasey thought. Everyone had told Jeanie, including Kasey herself, to stay away from him, that he'd only hurt her. "Glen may not have been someone that you or I would have chosen for Jeanie, but she loved him. In her own quiet way, she was just as stubborn as you and your father. Once she and Glen decided to drive to Mexico and get married, no one could have stopped them. Not you, not me, not your father."

"What the hell did my father care about her?" His words were filled with cold anger. "He expected perfection, in his horses, his employees, his children. Appearances were everything. That's why Jeanie ran away with Glen. My father would never have consented."

"It was a long time ago, Slater. People change."

"Jack Slater change?" He laughed dryly. "Not a chance in hell."

Slater was right, Kasey knew, that his father never would have agreed to a marriage between Jeanie and Glen. But she wasn't so certain that the man hadn't changed. She'd only spoken to him once since Jeanie's funeral, one day in town after her father had died. There was something different about him, something in his eyes, the tone of his voice, when he'd told her how sorry he was that her parents had died. He'd even apologized for not attending the services.

She looked at Slater now, remembering the man he was, knowing nothing about the man he'd become. He'd worked hard these past ten years, drifting from job to job, never staying in one place too long, careful not to let anyone too close. He didn't have to tell her, she could see it in his eyes, at the way he wouldn't look at her— really look at her—like she wanted him to. He'd come riding in like a knight in shining armor, ready to slay dragons. What she realized now was that he never took the armor off.

"Hey, Slate," she said, picking up a piece of hay and studying it, "remember my dad's fiftieth birthday party here at the house, and you brought Wendy Walker out to the barn?"

She watched the anger dissipate from his eyes, only to be replaced by a look of curious apprehension. "The way I remember it, Wendy dragged me out here."

"Right." She rolled her eyes, though she knew it was true. "Jeanie and I were already out here. I think we were fifteen at the time, and we'd sneaked a bottle of beer. We were going to split it when you and Wendy showed up."

He gave her a parental frown and she laughed. "Anyway, we ducked down behind the end stall, hoping you'd leave, but Wendy kept going on about how she'd heard how great you were with horses and how big your father's ranch was and she couldn't believe that some girl hadn't snatched you up yet."

Slater closed his eyes and shivered. "It's a recurring nightmare."

Kasey smiled. "And after every sentence she'd laugh, that special little trademark sound she was so famous for."

He groaned loudly. "The horse laugh."

"We used to call her Whinny Walker," Kasey said with a chuckle. "Not to her face, of course. She wasn't bad-looking, though with all that makeup it was hard to tell. So was she a good kisser?"

"I wouldn't know."

She twisted her body and stabbed at his chest with the piece of straw in her hand. "You kissed her. I saw you."

He shook his head. "Did not."

"Did, too." She nudged his arm with hers.

"Didn't." He nudged her back.

A nudge war started, with her insisting he had, and him insisting he hadn't. She wasn't sure who threw the first handful of hay, but they were both covered now, laughing and out of breath.

"I saw you. I remember every detail." Kasey gasped as Slater dumped another load of hay over her. She tossed it off, throwing her leg over Slater's thighs as she maneuvered into position for a counterattack. She had the advantage now. His body was underneath hers and she had an armload of ammunition. She let him have it.

"Yeah?" He sputtered and spit hay. "Just what do you remember?"

"Wendy wore a tight, black low-cut blouse. You wore a navy blue long-sleeved shirt. You were standing right

here, by this stall. She put her hands on your chest—"
Kasey slid her hands up Slater's chest "—and leaned in
real close."

Her deep breaths matched Slater's as she leaned into
him. She felt the rapid beating of his heart under the
palms of her hands, smelled the masculine scent of his
skin. His smile slowly faded as his gaze dropped to her
mouth.

"What else do you remember?" he murmured.

She couldn't remember anything. Not even her own
name. Heat rose from his body, and she felt as if she
were melting into him. She thought she should move
away, that she'd already taken this too far.

And then she didn't think at all.

Even as Kasey's lips brushed against his, Slater knew
he had to stop this. They were just messing around, teasing with each other, and somehow things had gotten out
of hand.

He reached up and wrapped his hands around her upper arms, intending to push her away.

He pulled her closer.

Damn, but she was sweet. Her mouth moved over his,
a soft, almost featherlike sensation that sent a wave of
heat down through the soles of his boots and back up
again. His hands tightened on her arms as he struggled
mentally with pushing her away or dragging her underneath him. When the tip of her tongue slid over his bottom lip, he found he couldn't move at all.

Okay, so maybe for the past four days he had wondered what it would be like to hold her like this, to kiss
her. But he'd sure as hell never planned on it happening;
he'd gone out of his way to avoid it. He'd been aware
of her since the moment he'd stepped into her house and
taken her in his arms. Even then, he'd felt something he

hadn't expected or wanted, a stirring deep in his gut that scared the hell out of him.

But this was *crazy,* he thought. Insane.

And it didn't matter. All that mattered was Kasey, her lips moving over his, the scent of peaches that drifted from her hair and skin, the press of her breasts against his chest.

The heat he'd felt only a second before was a raging inferno now. With a will of its own, his hand moved over her back, then raked upward, burying itself into her hair as he pulled her more tightly to him, deepening the kiss as he met her tongue with his own. The fact that she straddled his thighs and her body was pressed intimately with his intensified the need slicing through him.

Without breaking the kiss, he rolled her onto her back and pressed her into the hay as he spread his body beside hers. She moaned softly, a small whisper of need that sent his blood pounding in his temples. Her arms came around his neck and he leaned over her, slanting his mouth over hers again and again, murmuring her name with an urgency that shocked him.

She whimpered when his lips left hers, then sighed when his tongue found the wild pulse at the base of her throat. She arched her neck, dragging her fingers through his hair as she pulled him closer.

And when she moved against him, rubbing her thigh against his, he had to touch her. He *had* to.

Kasey thought she might die if he didn't touch her soon. Her body was on fire, blazing with the need consuming her. She'd wanted this, she'd wanted Slater, forever. From before that even, she was sure. She arched her body under his, not caring that he might think her brazen. At this moment, with this man, pleasure was all that mattered. To hell with pride. All pride would bring her was empty, cold longings of what could have been.

Her breath caught when his hand slid up her rib cage. *Yes, yes,* she thought, urging him silently. His lips, hot and moist, moved down her neck while his hand slid upward, slowly, too damn slowly. His knuckles lightly grazed the underside of her breast, and she cried out when his thumb skimmed the peak of one already hardened nipple. She cursed the cotton shirt and bra she had on, wanting nothing between her skin and Slater's touch. Could he hear her heart? she wondered. Could he not only hear it beating, but could he hear what it was saying to him? What it had always said to him?

It felt so right to be here with him, as if this was where she was meant to be, where she was always meant to be. She knew what it felt like now to truly be home, not only in this house, but here, with Slater. And even if it were only for this moment, for this tiny space in time, she would have this to cherish for all time.

But what of Slater? she thought suddenly. Would this be a moment for him to cherish, or a moment to regret? One more brick on the load he already carried on his shoulders. This would only be lust for him, a physical need satiated in a weak moment. He wasn't making love to her, he was losing himself and the past for a short while. And when the primal need was satisfied, he would come back to reality. She could deal with that, but could he?

No, she realized. He couldn't. And she didn't want him to remember her this way. With regrets.

To hell with reason, her body screamed at her, but her heart refused to listen.

"Slater," she whispered.

He answered by capturing her mouth again with an

urgency that left her reeling. His kiss was hard and deep, and in spite of herself, she responded with a low moan of pleasure. Her arms tightened around his neck—

No. Not like this.

With a silent curse, she loosened her arms and slid them away, fanning her hands across his chest as she gently pushed. It was like pressing against a concrete wall. Reluctantly she pulled her mouth from his.

"Slater." He opened his eyes when she called to him. She'd never seen them so dark, so intense. She shivered at the thrill that ran through her. "Slater, this is me, Kasey. I have to know if you realize that."

She saw the confusion, then the distress in his eyes before he closed them again tightly and rolled away from her.

"Kasey, my God." He sat slowly, raking his hands through his hair. "I'm sorry. I guess I got a little carried away."

Disappointed, she drew in a long breath and sat, keeping her shaky hands busy by picking hay out of her hair. Damn! She'd thrown herself at him, and he'd reacted like any red-blooded male. For her to think it was anything more than that was pure and simple fantasy. She had only herself to be angry at if things were suddenly awkward.

What the hell was she going to do now? What could she say?

She did the only thing she could think to do.

She laughed.

She pulled it from somewhere deep in her gut, a high-pitched, trembling equine sound that was as obnoxious as it was loud. The horses all stamped their hooves and snorted.

Startled, Slater froze, his eyes wide as he stared at Kasey as if she'd gone mad.

Then, slowly, a grin broke through the hard lines of his face. "Wendy," he said with a grimace.

"I told you that you kissed her."

He sighed with exasperation and shook his head. "No. She kissed me."

"Oh, I see." Kasey frowned at him. "You were the victim."

"I was," he said defensively. "What would you call being trapped with a woman who laughs like that?"

He did have a point. She stood and brushed the hay off her jeans, then picked up the rotted board Slater had pulled from the stall. "We'll let these babies grow up," she said, fitting the board back into place. "Then it's every mouse for himself."

He stood and shook the hay from his hair and clothes. "What about Miss Lucy?"

"She can go in the stall next door for now. It's not as big, but it's only temporary." She turned to him and jammed her hands into the front pockets of her jeans. His gaze met hers, held, and a long, strained moment passed between them.

"Well, good night," she said after a long moment, forcing her legs to move, praying that her knees wouldn't give out on her at least until she made it into the house.

"Hey, Kase."

She was almost to the barn door when he called her. He stood, watching her, his eyes narrowed, his expression grim.

"I just want you to know. I never kissed Wendy. Not like that."

She kept her eyes level with his and smiled slowly. "Yeah, Slate. I know."

She was whistling by the time she got to the house.

Five

The next morning Slater welcomed the sight of the large fallen sycamore branch beside the barn and eagerly set about the task of chopping it into firewood. Considering his frustration level after his encounter with Kasey in the barn last night, he probably could chew the limb into little stubs and spit them into a neat stack, but somehow an ax seemed a tad more civilized.

Not that he felt civilized. Even puppies and butterflies had best stay out of his way today.

And whose fault is it, Slater boy? that small voice of Reason whispered.

"Shut up," he grumbled.

With a savage swing, he brought the ax down on the base of the branch. It cracked loudly under the force of the blow and sent a reverberation up his arms that rattled his teeth. Wood chips flew and sparrows fluttering overhead scattered for safer territory.

What were you thinking? the voice persisted. *Or should I say, what were you thinking with?*

"Dammit, didn't I tell you to shut up?" Slater growled between his teeth as he swung the ax again.

Okay, so he had used the wrong part of his anatomy to think with last night. But when she'd kissed him, logic and good judgment left the building. What remained was pure and simple lust, he told himself. With her soft lips on his and that warm curvy body pressed against him, how the hell was he supposed to react?

Excuses, Reason chastised. *It was much more than lust, and you know it.*

"Don't be asinine," he snapped. He wasn't supposed to feel that way about Kasey. He *didn't* feel that way.

Did he?

No. He couldn't. They were friends. That's all. They'd grown up together, had some good times, some bad times. She'd just been kidding around last night and it got a little out of hand. They'd both laughed about it.

So why the hell had he gone to bed with the taste of her still in his mouth and the scent of her on his skin? And why the hell had his bed been a shambles this morning?

His hand tightened on the ax handle. Because he wanted her. He'd kept himself busy these past few days to avoid spending too much time with her and to keep his overactive imagination busy elsewhere, but the fact was, he wanted her. He'd wanted her in the barn, in his bed. He wanted her right now.

You can't have her, Reason dictated. *It's time for you to move on. Granite Ridge is not the place for you, and Kasey Donovan Morgan is certainly not the woman.*

"You think I don't know that?" he said irritably, and raised the ax over his head. Grunting loudly, he brought it down and the blade sliced all the way through the thickest part of the limb. The scent of fresh-cut wood filled the air.

And coffee.

He turned at the heavenly aroma and saw Cody and Troy sitting cross-legged by the edge of the barn, watching him work. Cody had a steaming mug of coffee on the ground in front of him.

"Hey, Slater, who you talkin' to?" Cody asked.

Damn, how long had they been sitting there? He racked his brain, trying to remember what he'd said and how many swear words he'd used. "No one."

"Sure you were. We heard you. Didn't we, Troy?"

Troy's cowlick waggled as he nodded earnestly.

With a flick of his wrist, Slater flung the ax and buried it into the limb. Hands on his hips, he walked over to the boys and frowned down at them. "You boys drinking coffee these days?"

Cody wrinkled his nose. "Nah. My mom sent it out for you. She's making breakfast and talking to herself, too."

Slater raised a brow. "Is that right?"

"She's grumpy, too," he complained. "She yelled at me just 'cause I spilled a drop of milk on the floor."

"Really?" Slater hunkered down beside the boys and picked up his coffee.

"Nuh-uh." Troy shook his head. "She yelled 'cause you tried to clean it up with the placemats on the table. And it wasn't a drop. You knocked over a whole glass with your baseball and she already told you not to bring it in the kitchen."

"She did not."

"Did, too."

"Okay, okay." Slater cut them off, knowing this could

go on for several minutes. "So she was talking to herself, huh?"

Cody and Troy both nodded. "Just like you. Only she had a wooden spoon she was swinging around instead of an ax."

"That serious, huh?" So Kasey was agitated this morning, too, was she? Slater took a thoughtful sip of his coffee. Could it be that their kiss had left her with the same frustration as him? She'd acted so casual about it last night, laughing it off like it was nothing.

He suddenly realized that was one of the reasons he'd been so testy himself this morning. It wasn't just his reaction that bothered him, but *her* reaction. He'd felt as if he'd been sucker punched, and she'd acted as if it was no more than a simple, innocent little smooch.

He smiled. So maybe he'd gotten to her just a little bit, too. It hardly made the situation any easier, but he couldn't deny his male pride was feeling a little less wounded.

"That was cool," Cody said. "The way you threw that ax and it stuck right in that old branch. We're going camping with Brian and his dad tomorrow night. Can we use that wood to build a fire on our trip?"

"This wood's too fresh," Slater said. "It has to cure first."

"Is it sick?" Troy asked.

Slater smiled. "That means it has to age and dry out before it can be used. There's some wood behind the barn that's ready now."

"You know how to pitch a tent?" Cody asked. "Mom found our grandpa's old tent in the barn, but there's a bunch of pieces and we don't know how to make it work."

Slater remembered helping Jared's brother, Jake, as-

BARBARA MCCAULEY 75

semble a bike for their eleven-year-old sister the night
before Christmas. It had taken all three Stone brothers
and himself until 2:00 a.m. before they finished. One little
tent shouldn't be too difficult. "We could probably figure
it out together."

Troy grinned brightly. "You sure know a lot of stuff."

Cody nodded in agreement. "His dad probably taught
him, like Brian's dad is always teaching him stuff, too."

Slater simply stared at the mug in his hand. His father
had taught him how to swing an ax, break a horse and
build a corral. But only because he'd have one less em-
ployee he'd have to pay. There'd never been camping
trips or baseball games or Saturday afternoons rebuilding
an engine. Work was the only thing Jack Slater had ever
known and the only thing he'd ever taught his children.

"Our dad moved to Mexico with Gloria." Troy made
circles in the dirt with his finger. "He sent us a postcard,
but says it's hard to call too much 'cause it's so far
away."

Mexico too far away? Hard to call? Where the hell
was their father living, in a cave? These were his kids,
dammit. They needed that phone call, needed to know he
gave a damn about them.

Slater's stomach twisted into a tight knot. What kind
of a bastard was this guy? He'd had a beautiful wife, two
fantastic kids and he walked away? More like crawled
away, Slater thought angrily. Based on Kasey's financial
struggles, Slater's guess was that Old Paul Baby was hid-
ing out.

"How far away is Alaska?" Troy asked. He'd found
a small rock in the dirt and deposited it into his pocket.

"Not too far to call," Slater said gently, knowing that
these kids needed so much more than a phone call.

"Too far to call where?"

Slater looked up at the sound of Kasey's voice. She stood at the edge of the barn, with morning light glinting fire off her auburn hair. She'd pulled it back this morning, but several wayward curls tumbled loose down her neck and over her shoulders. He wondered if he pulled his fingers through the thick strands if he'd find any remnants of hay.

"Alaska," Cody and Troy both answered at the same time.

"Slater says he's going to call us from there," Cody said. "Isn't that cool, Mom?"

"Cool." She glanced at him and he saw the rise of color on her cheeks. So there *was* something behind all that casual acceptance of the kiss they'd shared. When their eyes met, her cheeks darkened to a lovely shade of rose.

She slipped her hands into the back pockets of her jeans and quickly looked away. He looked away, too. The sight of her breasts pressed tightly against her white T-shirt had already sent his blood pressure up ten points.

"Breakfast is ready. Go wash up, boys."

Motivated by empty stomachs, they minded without an argument and ran off. Kasey watched them go, thinking how quickly they'd grown, how few years there really were left with them.

"They're great kids, Kase," Slater said. "You've done a hell of a job."

"Thanks, though sometimes I wonder who's doing a job on whom." She turned back to Slater with a smile. "What have you been doing out here?"

Cowardice had kept her in the kitchen all morning, when she'd really wanted to come out here to see what he was about with all that chopping. It was one thing to throw herself at him in the barn at night, and quite another to face him again in the light of day.

"You lost a branch during the night." He gestured toward the fallen limb.

Not to mention a whole lot of sleep, Kasey thought. Every time she closed her eyes, her mind replayed their kiss. Over and over and over. His lips moving over her neck, his hand skimming her back, her breast...

She blinked, realizing she was doing it again. Pretending interest, she walked over to the branch. "I see. So you felt compelled to chop it up for me."

"I don't know about compelled. It just needed to be done, so I did it."

"Lots of things need to be done." She tried to pull the ax out of the limb. It stuck tight. "That doesn't mean you need to do them. I appreciate the help, but this ranch is my responsibility. I need to know I can do it on my own."

Angry that she couldn't pull the ax out of the limb, she grabbed the handle with two hands. Setting her teeth, she dug her heels in and tugged as hard as she could. The ax came loose, and she went down on her butt.

Slater sat on the limb in front of her. Humiliated, she looked up at him and frowned. "Don't you dare say it."

"Say what?"

The amusement in his eyes infuriated her. She blew the bangs out of her eyes and struggled to recapture her pride. Sitting on the ground with dust swirling around her did make it somewhat difficult, though. "I have a chain saw somewhere," she declared, lifting her chin.

He lifted his brows. "Do you know how to use it?"

She knew he was teasing, but lack of sleep and a mountain of frustration had wiped out her sense of humor.

"No, I don't know how to use it. But then, I've had to do a lot of things in the past two years I've never done before." She hated herself for the moisture she suddenly felt burning her eyes. "Like telling the landlord that my husband cleaned out his side of the closet and our savings account at the same time. Then there was explaining to a four- and six-year-old their daddy wasn't coming back. That was a real education. And then there was—"

"Kasey." He sat beside her and gently slipped the ax from her hand. "Just in case you forget who you're talking to."

She laughed and laid her head on the shoulder he offered. "I'm sorry. I'm a little tired this morning."

He suspected that was his fault, but he hardly thought this was a good time to bring that up. "You want to tell me about it?"

"I'd say my little outburst just now pretty much summed it up."

He slid an arm around her shoulders and pulled her close. "Why don't you fill in a few details for me?"

She sighed, then sat straight and combed her fingers through her hair. "A year after Jeanie died, Paul was doing a story here in Granite Ridge on horse ranching. He interviewed my father, then asked me out. I'd just graduated high school and his life as a journalist seemed so exciting. I thought I wanted that excitement, to see the world, live every moment to its fullest. He stayed here for a few weeks after his assignment was finished, and in an impulsive moment we went to Vegas."

She remembered the ceremony and grimaced. A smoke-filled, fast-food-style wedding chapel had hardly been her dream, but Paul had promised a real wedding later. One with family and friends and flowers fresh out of the garden instead of plastic. She'd found out that later never came with Paul.

"We traveled a lot that first year," she went on. "It was fun, but not quite as exciting as I'd imagined. I was thrilled when I got pregnant with Cody, happy that we could finally settle down. Paul wanted no part of the baby. He even told me to get rid of it."

Slater's arm tightened around her shoulders. He cursed, something raw and crude, and she nodded in agreement.

"That's pretty close to what I said when I left him. I came back here and told my parents I was just visiting for a while, though I think they suspected something was wrong.

"Paul called three weeks later and sent flowers, apologizing and begging me to come back. Said I'd just surprised him and he'd gotten used to the idea now. What I didn't know then was that Paul had found out his boss was a family man. Promotions and raises and the best stories went to the men with families. Cody wasn't even six months old when he started in on me to have another child. I didn't mind. I'd wanted several. The fact that my marriage wasn't so wonderful didn't even matter to me, as long as I had my children. I almost think I was relieved when he left. It forced me to face the truth and get on with my life."

"I could break his legs, if you'd like," Slater offered politely.

She laughed. "I might have said yes that first year. Getting a good job, finding sitters, dealing with car repairs and backed-up plumbing." She picked up the ax again and swung it into the branch. It didn't go in as deeply as Slater's throw, but at least it stuck. "I know now he actually did me a favor by leaving. I learned how to manage by myself, and when I'd saved enough money to bring this place back to life, I sold my car, bought a truck and moved back here. End of story.''

''Sounds more like the beginning to me,'' Slater said thoughtfully.

''It is. Not just for me, but for Cody and Troy, too. There's been a lot of adjustments, but we've settled down. This is our home now and we love it here. They start school on Tuesday, they'll make more friends, and before long I'm going to have every stable full of champion quarter horses.''

He took her chin in his hand and lifted her face to his.

''I believe you, Acacia Donovan,'' he said quietly. ''I admire you.''

His words brought a fullness to her heart. She looked at him and there was something in his eyes she'd never seen before; a softness that made her insides go hot and cold at the same time. His hand felt rough against her skin, his fingers warm and gentle. This was the Slater she remembered. The Slater she'd fallen in love with when she was thirteen years old.

The Slater she was still in love with.

His breath fell on her cheek, his lips, so close to hers, were set in a firm line. His fingers slowly tightened on her chin, and her heart began to pound furiously as he lowered his mouth to hers.

A horn blared, long and loud and very close. They jumped apart.

''Mom! Mom!'' The back door slammed. ''Miss Lucy's here!''

They had a celebration breakfast picnic in the barn. Cody and Troy spread out an old blanket while Kasey unloaded the basket of food. Slater brought paper plates, napkins and silverware, then filled plastic cups with sparkling apple juice. The guest of honor stood crunching oats, watching curiously from her stall, no doubt wondering what all the fuss was about.

"To Miss Lucy." Kasey raised her glass. "Welcome to the Double D."

"To Miss Lucy!" Cody and Troy mimicked. Cups touched all around.

Miss Lucy swished her tail. The gray in stall two gave a loud snort and the chestnut stamped a hoof.

Smiling, Slater sat back and enjoyed the festivities with Kasey and her sons. Breakfast on a blanket in a barn, he thought with amusement, munching on a piece of bacon. A first.

"Isn't Miss Lucy the most beautiful horse you ever seen?" Cody asked Slater.

"Saw." Kasey handed her son a napkin. "And you have strawberry jam on your nose."

"A drop-dead knockout." Slater agreed with Cody. He'd checked the mare out carefully while Kasey signed the necessary papers. The horse was a gorgeous little sorrel with a blaze of white up her nose and huge brown eyes. Based on her lines and formation, she'd make one hell of a broodmare.

"What's a drop-dead knockout?" Troy asked around a huge bite of toast.

"Well, let's see." Slater squinted thoughtfully and scratched at his neck. "It's more than beautiful. It's incredibly gorgeous, make-your-eyes-pop-out, stunning, dazzling and absolutely exquisite."

Troy used his finger to stuff in another bite of toast. "Like my mom."

"Yeah." Slater grinned and looked at Kasey. Her cheeks flushed. "Exactly like your mom."

"Yeah," Cody joined in. "Just like you, Mom. You're a knockout."

She arched one brow suspiciously, but her green eyes had brightened with pleasure. "Why do I feel as if there's more getting buttered up here than the toast? What is it you boys want?"

I want you. The thought popped into Slater's head before he could stop it. *In my bed, your bed. Anywhere I can get you.*

He cursed himself and pushed the image out of his mind. Wanting and having were two different things. And besides, hadn't he already had this discussion with himself just a little while ago?

"Slater said he'd show us how to pitch Grandpa's tent," Cody said. "Troy and me thought we could set it up in the barn and sleep here tonight. Then we'd be real experts when we go on our camping trip tomorrow night. And besides, Miss Lucy might be lonely, this being her first night away from her friends and all. We could keep her company."

"You want to sleep out here?" Kasey asked incredulously. "All night, in the barn, by yourselves? No television?"

"Jeez, Mom," Cody huffed with exasperation. "We're not babies."

"Yeah, Mom," Troy added, but Kasey saw the tiny worry line on her younger son's brow as he glanced around the barn.

She shuddered at the thought of spiders and mice and all the creepy crawlies that slithered out at night.

"Come on, Mom," Cody persisted. "We're not scared. Slater, tell her it's okay. Tell her we're not babies."

"Sure, Kase. They're big boys."

Kasey frowned as she looked at Slater. He was busy balancing a paper plate in one hand and maneuvering a forkful of scrambled eggs into his mouth with the other. Some help he was.

Outnumbered, she sighed with resignation. Cody and Troy, knowing they'd won, whooped and hollered and began listing supplies to gather up.

Lord help her, she thought as her gaze landed on Slater's crooked grin and her heart skipped a beat, the male sex was going to be the death of her yet.

Slater had barely finished driving the final stake into the ground that afternoon before Cody and Troy were inside the tent unloading the stash of supplies they'd been gathering all day, including, but not limited to: flashlight, compass, slingshot, bottled water, baseball cards, rock collection, comic books and a bagful of action heroes. They'd holed up inside their shelter the rest of the day, coming in long enough to inhale some dinner, reluctantly help with the cleanup, then fill their pockets with Extra Sour Fruity Flavored Snappy Tarts and tear out the back door again. Troy was halfway to the barn when he ran back and deposited a handful of the soft chewy candy on the counter, gave Kasey a kiss, then Slater a high five before he ran out after his brother.

Slater went upstairs to take a shower, and she began to pace.

The sun had gone down. She peeked out the back door and turned the porch light on. The barn door was open and she saw the eerie flicker of the flashlight in the darkness.

Slater had laughed at her, spouting off something about male rites of passage or some such hogwash, then made her promise not to go out and check up on them—at least not until they were asleep. He'd even made her cross her heart, for heaven's sake.

But it was dark. There were insects out there. Small animals. Spooky noises.

Chewing intently on a fingernail, she glanced up at the ceiling. She could hear the water from the shower running overhead. She lost her train of thought for a moment, thinking about Slater up in her bathroom, naked, soaping up that tall, muscular body of his. She quickly shook the thought, though not before a shot of heat rippled up her spine.

What harm could it do to sneak a peek? Not at Slater, she thought with a sly smile. At her sons. They wouldn't even have to know. She could be very quiet. And if they caught her, she'd simply tell them that...that she was bringing them more batteries. In case the flashlight burned out.

Satisfied with that story, she popped a red and yellow fruity tart into her mouth, then dug through the pantry and found two D batteries. She'd be back in a flash, and who'd be the wiser?

She shut the porch light off before she opened the back door. She didn't want them to see her in case they looked out. Slowly, quietly, she closed the door behind her.

She hadn't gone more than ten feet before her boot caught a rock and she stumbled, dropping the batteries. Damn. Why couldn't there at least be a little moonlight tonight? she thought irritably and sank to her knees. She patted the ground blindly, but felt only grass under her hands. How far away could batteries roll on grass?

The air had already started to cool, and she worried her sons wouldn't be warm enough. Maybe she should go back and get an extra blanket for them. An extra pair of socks.

She found one battery, then the other, and shoved them into her front pocket. She stood and brushed off her knees, then turned quickly toward the barn.

And ran smack-dab into a very large, very solid man.

Six

"And just what exactly are you doing out here?" He steadied her by grabbing hold of her shoulders.

"Slater." She sucked in a startled breath. Good Lord, the man had dressed quickly. "I thought you were in the shower."

"For shame, Acacia," he said imperiously. "Didn't you cross your heart?"

Cody and Troy might buy her story of the batteries, but she knew that Slater wouldn't. "I was, uh, well, I just remembered that—"

He clucked his tongue and pulled her deeper into the shadows by the back porch. When she started to protest, he shushed her. A burst of high-pitched laughter from the barn had her turning, but he held her tight.

"They're having a good time, Kase," he whispered. "Stop worrying."

Frowning, she listened to the sound of their play. "It's just so dark out here."

"Exactly. And as soon as they realize just how dark it is, they'll be walking, or more likely running, right back into the house. I give them about ten more minutes. Fifteen tops."

She thought about that. Of course, she realized, feeling ridiculous. Slater was absolutely right. Troy would be the first to cave in, and Cody would be right behind him. "When did you get so smart about little boys?"

"When I was eight, Tommy Johnson and I didn't last forty-five minutes out in his backyard. He swore he saw a devil dog, with horns and eyes that spit fire. Turned out his sister's pet goat got loose."

He chuckled at the memory, and she felt the rumble deep in his chest. A very strong, broad chest, she noted, suddenly aware of his closeness. Concern for her sons faded, and in its place was a growing warmth where Slater's hands held her arms. A warmth that was spreading through her entire body.

He *had* dressed quickly, she realized. His black T-shirt felt slightly damp, as did his skin. The clean, fresh smell of the soap he'd used drifted to her, mingling with the musky scent of his shampoo.

"Well, I guess I should go in now." She heard the breathless sound of her own voice, felt the low, steady thud of her heart. She made no move to leave.

"You should." He made no move to let her go.

She wasn't sure what happened first, if her hands slid over his shoulders, or his moved down her back. She wasn't sure if she lifted her face to his first, or he lowered his.

She didn't care.

Parting her lips, she met the gentle touch of his mouth

against hers. Pleasure swirled like a hot wind through her, seeping into every vein, every pore. His hand tightened on her back, then moved lower, cupping her bottom as he pulled her closer. She eagerly met the thrust of his tongue, and when he deepened the kiss she raked her hands upward through his wet hair and held on, wanting more, needing more.

"Strawberry...no, lemon," he said hoarsely, dragging his mouth over her chin, then down her neck. He hadn't shaved, and the stubble of his beard felt like tiny pricks of electricity on her sensitive skin. With a low growl, he caught her mouth again, consuming her with his lips and tongue. Her pulse pounded wildly; her head swam; her entire body ached.

"Strawberry-lemon," he decided, nearly lifting her off the ground to fit her body more intimately to his. He held her to him, nearly crushing her, and she shuddered from the intensity of desire that rocked her, from the rigid need she felt pressing against her hip and at the juncture of her thighs...

What?

Something seemed to be anatomically incorrect here, she thought dimly, trying to sort through the confusion. The stiff bulge pressing against her hipbone was separate from the bulge pressing between her legs.

The batteries.

She couldn't help it. Even though he was still kissing her, she started to laugh. She tried to stop it, but she just couldn't. The batteries, for heaven's sake!

He went still, then slowly pulled his mouth from hers. "I'm beginning to get a real complex every time I kiss you, Kase. You wanna share the joke with me?"

She put one hand on his chest to steady herself, then smothered her laughter with the other. "It's just that I—"

she sucked in a breath. "I forgot that I had these in my pocket—" a fresh wave of giggles started in "—and I got a little confused and—" She took his hand and brought it to her pocket, then broke up again.

She heard him draw in a deep breath and swear lightly, then he began to laugh, too. They sank to the ground, each of them shushing the other, when suddenly a light blasted them in the face.

"What's so funny?" Cody asked, aiming his flashlight directly into Slater's eyes. Troy stood beside his brother, candy bag in one hand, action heros in the other.

"Nothing much." Slater reached out and inched the flashlight away, directing the beam of light off his face. "What's up with you boys?"

Cody and Troy glanced at each other. "Nothin' much," Cody said hesitantly. "We was just taking a little hike to, uh, stretch our legs."

"A little hike into the house?" Slater stood and helped Kasey up.

"Just to get some more supplies," Cody defended. "We, uh, ran out of water."

"Well, then," Kasey said, brushing off her jeans, "we better get you a drink before you dehydrate. I'll bet I could even whip us up some root beer floats, if you're real thirsty."

With a whoop of pleasure, Cody and Troy raced up the back steps. She watched them try to knock each other over as they pushed through the door and disappeared into the house.

"Go ahead, say it." She turned to Slater and smiled. "I believe the words are, 'I told you so.'"

He said nothing, just combed his hands through his damp hair and pulled in a deep breath. "Kasey," he said after a long, awkward moment. "I'm leaving tomorrow."

She looked at him through the darkness that suddenly seemed to close in on her. Of course he was leaving. He'd stayed longer than she'd ever thought he would. She should be happy about that, satisfied with the time they'd had together. She should be, but dammit, she wasn't.

"Call of the wild, huh?" She ignored the tightening in her chest and forced a lightness in her voice. "Glaciers, salmon fishing, caribou. The primeval need to be one with nature."

"I think we both know why I'm leaving," he said evenly. "It has nothing to do with Alaska, and everything to do with primeval needs."

Her cheeks warmed at his candid explanation. "That's no reason to leave, Slate. We're both adults."

"Adults who are mutually attracted to each other, and would be alone for the next two days."

She took a step toward him, shocked by the invitation she was so blatantly offering. "And that frightens you?"

He gave a dry, short laugh. "Hell, Kase, it terrifies me. I admit it. I want you. I want you in my bed and underneath me so bad it hurts. If it hadn't been for two little boys, that's where you'd be right now."

His words sent a thrill up her spine, followed by sharp disappointment.

"Kasey." He released a long, slow breath. "You deserve a hell of a lot more than I could ever give you. You and the boys deserve someone who will be there for you tomorrow, and the day after that. Someone who can make promises and keep them. Granite Ridge and the Double D, those are your dreams. You belong here. I don't."

"No one's shut the corral gate." She swallowed back the thickness in her throat. "You can leave anytime you want."

Frustrated, angry and more than a little embarrassed, she turned and headed for the house. Rejection was never an easy pill to swallow.

"Kasey."

She paused at the back door, but didn't turn around.

"I don't want to hurt you," he said quietly.

She almost laughed at the absurdity of it all. He hadn't wanted to hurt her ten years ago, either. The man was just as blind now as he was then.

And she was just as big a fool.

Her hand tightened on the doorknob, then, head straight, shoulders squared, she went into the house and drank root beer floats with her sons.

"Lord have mercy! Hugh Slater! It really is you!"

With a silent groan, Slater glanced up from the row of fishing rods he'd been studying and saw Mrs. Agatha Hepple, his seventh-grade teacher, strutting toward him with the same enthusiasm she'd always used to lead the Granite Ridge Marching Band.

"MaryAnn Milberry told me she saw you here in the sporting goods section," she said, waving a black purse at him as if it were a baton. "But I told MaryAnn she must be wrong. I told her that Hugh Slater would have come seen me first thing if he'd come back to town."

Slater tugged the brim of his Stetson lower and smiled tightly as he watched the well-rounded woman approach. She was gray around the temples now, but the glasses were the same, as was the rosy blush on her apple cheeks. He'd been in town no more than thirty minutes and twenty-five had already been spent with hellos and where-have-you-been-for-ten-years?

Exactly the reason he'd chosen not to come to town for the past week. But when Cody and Troy had asked him to come into Granite Ridge and help them pick out new hiking boots for their camping trip, it was impossible to say no. Besides, he'd wanted to spend a little extra time with them before they left.

Before he left.

Which would be right after Kasey dropped her sons off at Brian's house this afternoon.

"I declare," Mrs. Hepple exclaimed, "you've grown at least three more inches, Hugh. You always were the tallest boy in Granite Ridge. I believe you still are."

He glanced to the opposite end of the aisle, hoping for escape, but MaryAnn Milberry, the assistant librarian, had rounded the corner.

Trapped.

They fired questions at him, not really bothering to let him answer before they interrupted each other. He simply stood back and endured the examination, shaking his head or shrugging. MaryAnn was certain she'd heard he'd gone to work for the railroads, and Mrs. Hepple argued that he'd been on the rodeo circuit.

He caught sight of Kasey and the boys at the end of the aisle and inclined his head for her to come rescue him. She simply stood there, looking pretty in a long floral skirt and white V-necked cotton top and smiled at him, her eyes sparkling with amusement as she watched the entertainment. In spite of himself, and even with Mrs. Hepple and MaryAnn clucking over him, he felt his breath catch at the sight of her.

"Did you know that Hugh here played the bass drum in seventh grade?" Mrs. Hepple boasted.

Pressing his lips tightly together, he widened his eyes and looked at Kasey again. Her grin widened and he frowned. If this was her revenge for the havoc he'd caused in her life, it was definitely working. Cody and Troy had moved closer and were listening intently.

"Well," MaryAnn said, strolling down memory lane with Mrs. Hepple, "Hugh was always my best reader at the library. I still remember he checked out *Robinson Crusoe* ten times before I finally gave the boy the book myself. Do you still read the classics, my dear? Kasey Donovan, is that you? Land sakes, child, what's all this talk about you advertising for a husband?"

It was Slater's turn to grin now. Kasey's cheeks turned bright red as the attention suddenly shifted to her.

"It was a misunderstanding," Kasey explained, frowning at Slater.

"You didn't need to place an ad, dear." Mrs. Hepple patted her arm. "In fact, my cousin's boy, Marcus, he runs the bait shop and—"

"Worm Boy?" MaryAnn rolled her eyes. "For heaven's sake, Aggie, he's hardly husband material for our little Kasey. Now, take my nephew's brother, Simon, he's just the perfect—"

"Mrs. Hepple, MaryAnn," Kasey broke in. "Thank you for your concern, but truly, I'm not looking for a husband."

"Well, you should be." MaryAnn offered her omniscient opinion. "A beautiful young woman like you, living alone—"

"I'm not alone." Kasey slid an arm around each of her son's shoulders and smiled down at them. "I have Cody and Troy."

"And two fine boys, they are." MaryAnn beamed at

the youngsters. "Why haven't they been to the library yet?"

Kasey looked truly contrite. "It's been a busy summer."

"Yeah, real busy," Cody offered. "Mom took us on a neat vacation and we rode on a roller coaster and went to a rodeo and Slater's been staying with us ever since."

It was like a still frame in an old slide movie. Silence, then slowly, eyebrows lifted, Mrs. Hepple and MaryAnn turned toward Slater.

"Slater was just passing through," Kasey interjected quickly. "I asked him to take a look at a mare I bought."

Slater could almost see the gears working furiously in Mrs. Hepple's and MaryAnn's brains. Dammit! This was exactly the other thing he'd wanted to avoid: the townspeople ruminating about his involvement with Kasey. Not that he had an involvement, he thought grimly. But with him staying at her place, there would most certainly be speculation.

He touched the brim of his hat, knowing the time to escape was now, before the women could gather their wits. "Mrs. Hepple, MaryAnn. It's been a pleasure."

Taking hold of Kasey's elbow, he quickly whisked her toward the checkout counter. He never should have let them be seen together. It had been selfish of him to come here with her, to give in to the need he'd felt to spend a little more time with her. Now the whole damn town would be talking, and Kasey would be left to suffer for his foolishness.

And even still, as he held on to her elbow, an elbow that he should have let go of three aisles back, he was glad he was here with her. She not only looked real pretty in that skirt, but she smelled pretty, too. Not peaches this time, but something else just as light and sweet. When the boys ran ahead to check out the candy shelves, and Kasey paused at the magazine rack, he looked both ways to make sure the aisle was clear, then gave in to the need twisting in his gut.

Shoving his hands casually into his pockets, he stepped behind her and leaned down, brushing his nose close to her neck. He breathed in deeply, closing his eyes as he drew the intoxicating scent into his lungs. Damn, but this woman was the stuff fantasies were made of. His fantasies. He thought about that skirt; how easily it would slide up those long legs of hers, how silky her skin would feel underneath, how soft her thighs—

"Slater! Hugh Slater! It *is* you!"

He jumped back, not only furious that he'd been interrupted in his daydream, but guilty that he'd been caught. When he saw who'd called his name, it was all he could do not to run the other way.

Wendy Walker.

She came at him as if she were a linebacker and he had the ball. Her ample bosom, half exposed by the deep scoop of her tight black top, collided with his chest as she threw her arms around him. If he'd been a shorter man, she'd have smothered him with her cleavage. Tolerating the hug, he looked around the blonde's skyscraper hairdo and saw Kasey struggling not to laugh. He'd get her for this, he thought, fuming. How could she stand there and laugh at him while he was being mauled by this Amazon?

"Slater, oh, Slater, how wonderful to see you," Wendy crooned.

"Yeah, Wendy." He pried her arms off his neck and smiled tightly. "Uh, you, too."

Wendy's bright red lips pouted and one long tipped, glossy white fingernail tapped him on his chest. "How naughty of you not to call me. Did you just get into town?''

''Well, I, it's been a couple—''

''A whole week now, isn't it, Slate?'' Kasey offered. ''Hello, Whinny—uh, Wendy.''

Wendy's smile dipped as she looked at Kasey, then back to Slater. ''A whole week? But I was just at your dad's ranch three days ago, measuring his office for new blinds. I own my own decorating business now,'' she said proudly, then snapped open her leopard-skin purse— which happened to match her skintight pants—and began to dig through it. ''Walker's Interiors.''

She slipped a business card into Slater's front jeans' pocket. ''That's my home phone on the bottom left corner. Oh, and Kasey—'' she handed a card to her, also ''—put this in your phone book and call me when you're ready to do some remodeling.''

Kasey politely dropped it into her purse, knowing exactly where it was going when she got home. She wouldn't let Wendy change a lightbulb in her house, let alone decorate.

She pressed her lips tightly together, fighting down the little green monster that reared its head as Wendy sidled up to Slater. What was the point in jealousy? He was leaving. Today. As soon as they dropped Cody and Troy off at Brian's, they'd drive back to the ranch and he'd leave. She knew his bag was sitting on the floor in the guest room, and last night, after the boys had come in from outside, he'd gone out in the garage and worked on his truck. Preparing it for the long trip, most likely.

Or, more likely, staying as far away from her as he could.

Just thinking about their kiss last night brought a wave of heat up her neck. He'd told her he wanted her, but she wasn't sure now. Based on her own behavior, and now Wendy's, no doubt Slater was used to women throwing themselves at him. Maybe he'd just been trying to soften his rejection. The same way he was being so nice to Wendy right now. Smiling at her and staring down at her chest.

"So if you're not staying with your father, then where are you staying?" Wendy asked Slater, her hand glued to his arm as she leaned into him.

"He's staying with me," Kasey blurted before Slater could answer, cursing herself for sounding so possessive. Wendy's eyes opened so wide Kasey could have sworn that the woman's mascara had cracked.

"Oh, of course," Wendy said, looking from Kasey back to Slater. "Your little sister was Kasey's best friend. But if you needed a place to stay, you should have called me. Since my divorce, my house just seems so big, and I do have a spare bedroom."

Of course, Wendy's look said that they wouldn't have needed it, Kasey noted.

"At least stop by and see me," Wendy went on. "We can talk about old times and all the laughs we used to have."

"Funny you should mention that," Kasey said, even though she saw the warning look from Slater. "Just the other night, Slater and I were reminiscing about that very thing."

"Were you?" Delighted, Wendy gave a little bounce. "Slater, you were talking about me?"

"A regular chatterbox, he was. It's amazing that a man could remember such detail about a woman after all those years." The violence in Slater's eyes should have stopped her, but she was on a roll now. And quite frankly, she didn't give a damn. "Excuse me, will you? My sons are waiting for me at the checkout."

She ducked out, but not before the loud, braying sound of a horse in pain rang through the store. Biting her lower lip, she quickly paid for her sons' new boots and several candy bars, then hurried out the front door of the store and leaned against the wall, waiting for Slater while Cody and Troy dug through the candy. It wasn't thirty seconds before Slater was standing over her with a murderous expression on his face and his hands on his hips.

"Dammit, Kasey," he snarled, "that wasn't funny."

She looked up at him innocently, trying to be serious, but her lips twitched traitorously.

"It wasn't," he insisted, but she could see the corners of his mouth flicker, too. He leaned against the store wall with her, and when Kasey imitated Wendy's laugh perfectly, he jammed his hat low on his head and struggled to keep his own laughter in.

"Okay, so maybe it was a little funny." He began to chuckle. "But if I have any more nightmares, it's going to be your fault."

"Hello, Hugh."

The laughter died in Slater's throat at the sound of the familiar voice. The smile left his face as he slowly lifted his head and gazed into eyes the same deep brown as his own.

"Hello, Father."

Seven

Slater suddenly understood what it must feel like to be a bug caught up in a vacuum. One minute you're just tooling along, minding your own business, the next you're sucked up into a dark place and you can't breath. Ignoring the clutch in his gut, he straightened until his gaze was level with the man standing in front of him.

His father hadn't changed much, Slater thought, though silver streaked his temples and mustache, and the lines around his eyes had deepened. Jack Slater had always been an imposing figure, the kind of man whose authority was rarely questioned, the kind of man whose rangy build, broad shoulders and large hands welcomed a hard day's labor and expected the same from everyone else. Horses and ranching were all he'd ever known. All he'd ever cared about.

They faced each other, neither moving, assessing. Remembering.

"I heard you were back," Jack said finally.

Slater shook his head. "Not back. Just passing through."

There was something in his father's eyes, a strange glint that was gone as quickly as it came. "Where you staying?"

"At Kasey's." He no longer had to explain himself to this man or give reasons. But it made no difference to tell his father where he'd been staying. He'd know soon enough, anyway.

Jack glanced behind Slater and touched the brim of his white cowboy hat. "I heard you'd moved back a few weeks ago, Kasey. These your boys?"

Kasey stepped forward, a hand on each of her sons' shoulders. "Cody, Troy, this is Mr. Slater."

Wide-eyed, Cody and Troy studied the older man carefully, then Cody asked, "Are you really Slater's dad?"

"Yeah, son." Jack looked at Slater. "That I am."

His father's voice had always been rough and smoke-graveled, but there seemed a smoother edge to it now, Slater noted. Certainly not soft, but subdued somehow. He noticed there were no cigarettes in the pocket of his blue work shirt and wondered if he'd given up smoking.

"The boys have to be somewhere," Slater said after a moment's silence.

"We're going camping with Brian and his dad," Troy offered.

"That a fact." Jack tipped his hat back. "Brian Turner?"

Surprise lit Cody's eyes. "You know Brian?"

"Sure do." Jack nodded. "Know his daddy, too. He's a fine doctor."

Slater glanced at his father. A compliment from Jack Slater? Brian's father must be one hell of a doctor.

There were people staring. Slater knew that. Passing cars slowed down, faces peered from store windows, shoppers on the street stopped or walked with a snail's pace. Everyone watching. It was no secret to Granite Ridge that Hugh Slater and his father had been estranged for ten years. There was a drama unfolding here, right in front of Helman's Department Store. Before the sun went down, there wouldn't be a citizen within ten miles who hadn't heard one version or another of the encounter. Slater didn't much give a damn one way or the other. The only thing he really minded was dragging Kasey into it.

He drew in a slow breath and pulled his hat low. "We have to go."

"Come by the ranch, Hugh."

Slater hesitated, then shook his head slowly. "I'm leaving after Kasey and I drop the boys off. I've got a job in Alaska."

Jack opened his mouth, then closed it again, pressing his lips tightly together as he nodded. He looked at Kasey. "Bring the boys by sometime, Kasey. I've got some ponies that need some exercise."

Faces bright with hope, Cody and Troy looked at their mother. "Thank you, Mr. Slater. I'll do that."

He walked away, a hitch in his stride that Slater had never seen before.

Ignoring Kasey's steady gaze, Slater turned and walked in the opposite direction.

The boys were too excited about their first camping trip to notice the tension in the truck on the drive from town to Brian's house, but for once, Kasey welcomed her

sons' endless chatter. She understood that Slater needed
a little time to absorb the meeting with his father, just as
she needed time to prepare herself for the solitude she
faced for the next two days. It was bad enough that Cody
and Troy would be gone, but with Slater leaving, too, she
was looking forward to the quiet with the same enthusiasm as an appendectomy.

And after the boys had waved goodbye from the back
seat of Brian's father's Jeep Cherokee and she and Slater
were pulling into her driveway, Kasey decided definitely
that an operation *would* be easier.

She'd barely parked the truck before he got out and
headed for the house, his stride measured, his face im-
passive. She sat very still and watched him for a moment,
then drew in a long, slow breath and followed him inside.

She found him in the upstairs bedroom, bent over his
open duffel bag, packing the toiletries he'd picked up at
the drugstore in town.

"If I leave now," he said, stuffing a can of shaving
cream into a small leather pouch, "I might make Amarillo before it gets dark."

She checked the dresser drawer he'd been using, but
it was empty. "You might even have time to stop and
see your father."

"I've seen my father."

She closed the drawer and leaned back against the
dresser. "You haven't talked to him."

He zipped up the leather pouch with a snap of his wrist
and tossed it into the bag. "My father and I never talked,
Kasey. We fought. I sure as hell didn't come back here
after ten years to get into another argument with him."

"Oh, yes, that's right." It was impossible to keep the
sarcasm out of her voice. "You came here to rescue me

from marriage. To talk some sense into this foolish little brain of mine.''

His eyes narrowed as he straightened. ''Are you just trying to make me mad, or do you have a point here?''

''I have two points. Number one is that things are not always what they seem on the surface. You were wrong about me, maybe you're wrong about your father. He asked you to come see him, Slater. That wasn't easy for him.''

''He didn't ask me to come by. He told me to.''

She wanted to throttle him. Instead, she rolled her head back and groaned at the ceiling. ''Slater, for God's sake, he took the first step, it's your turn now.''

Slater hoisted the duffel bag on his shoulder and stared at her. ''You had a second point.''

He wasn't listening to a word she said. She hadn't wanted their goodbye to be like this. She'd imagined a tender hug, maybe even a chaste kiss and a smile. All very civilized and adult. Motherhood and a marriage gone sour had evened her temper long ago, taught her patience and control. She had no intention of letting Hugh Slater blow in and out of her life and shoot all that hard-earned patience and control to hell.

That's what she told herself every step as she closed the distance between them and stood in front of him, blocking his way.

''You came back here because you felt an obligation to save me from making a mistake, at least that's what you told yourself. You thought you could make peace with your past by doing something noble with the present.''

She saw the intensity in his dark eyes, the jump of a muscle in his temple. To hell with control, she decided. To hell with patience. The man she loved was leaving and if she couldn't give him her heart, then she'd most certainly give him a piece of her mind.

She leaned in closer still, close enough to feel the heat of his emotions rising, and lifted her face to his. "But all those grand intentions blew up in your face when you found out that you were physically attracted to me. Never in a hundred years would you have expected what's happened between us, what's happening right now. The fact is, the reason you're racing out of here is not because of your father, but because it scares the hell out of you to be alone with me. It scares the hell out of me, too. But at least I can admit it. At least I'm not running away from it."

His face was like granite, his words as hard and cold. "I can't give you what you want, Kase."

She curled her hands into fists at her sides, and locked eyes with his. "You don't have a clue what it is I want. No more than you know what you want."

She turned then, determined to walk away and salvage what little dignity she could. The speed with which he grabbed her upper arm made her breath catch in her throat, and when he pulled her up against his hard body, her lips parted in a soft gasp of surprise.

"That's where you're wrong, Kasey." His gaze burned into hers. "I know exactly what I want."

The duffel bag fell to the floor with a loud thump as he covered her still-parted lips with his mouth. His kiss was savage, hungry, his grip on her arms painful. He devoured her, and she answered him, circling his broad shoulders with her arms, lifting herself up even as she pulled him down to her.

This is what had been between them since the night he'd shown up at her doorstep. Deep inside each other, a slumbering beast, waiting for the moment—this moment—to break its chains and escape. A mixture of excitement and fear coursed through her, for now that the beast was loose, could it be controlled? And did they want to control it? She gasped as he lifted her completely off the floor and into his arms as if she weighed no more than a feather.

What was the adage? Be careful what you wish for, because you might get it? Perhaps, she thought dimly. But regrets she would deal with later, and later would come only too soon.

She clung to him, twisting her body against his, needing him closer. He accommodated her, cupping her buttocks, then guiding her legs around his waist. She moaned at the intimate touch of their bodies, his tongue mating with hers, her breasts against his solid chest, the bold press of his manhood against the juncture of her thighs. A fire of need swept through her, dancing over her skin and skipping across her senses.

He slanted his mouth against hers over and over, his kisses hot and deep, edged with a desperation that she understood only too well. A storm raged between them, a tempest as dark as it was sensual. She reveled in the sensations that exploded through her and shamelessly ran her hands up his neck and through his hair, digging her nails into his scalp as she pulled him closer still.

The distance to the bed was a mere foot, but for Kasey it felt as if she'd traveled the longest journey of her life, a journey that was bringing her home, to the place where she was always meant to be. She smiled at the sound of her name on his lips, his murmur of need, then his low moan of satisfaction when he pressed her back against the bed.

Her hands were free now and she made quick use of them, spreading her fingers over his chest, then downward, tugging his shirt from his jeans. His lips moved over her jaw, then down her neck...her throat, trailing moist hot kisses, searing her skin with his tongue and teeth.

The mattress dipped as he knelt over her on the bed, his gaze intense as he slipped off her flats then skimmed his hands upward, baring her calves, her knees, her thighs. Her breath caught, then held as his thumbs caressed the soft skin of her inner thighs, moving slowly upward, to the core of her heat. She closed her eyes, awash in the erotic whisper of his hands. He bent over her, his hands gently kneading, the tips of his fingers skimming the lace edge of her panties with feather softness.

She heard the sound of her own whimper, then his sharp intake of breath as he pushed her top upward and unclipped the front clasp of her bra, exposing her breasts. His gaze feasted hungrily on her, and she saw his eyes darken and narrow as he cupped the soft flesh in his hands. His thumbs made slow circles over the rosy tips of her breasts, then he lowered himself to her and drew the hardened peak of one nipple into his mouth.

Her heart slammed in her chest, and her fingers dug into the bedspread as his hot, wet tongue swirled over her. She arched upward, whimpering as he worked his magic on her. His palms were rough, and the texture on her sensitive skin sent ripples of pleasure through every nerve.

He raised his head, and the fierce, savage look in his eyes brought a shiver to her. He hauled himself to his knees and straddled her, keeping his dark gaze locked on hers as he tugged his shirt off, then unbuckled his belt and slid the zipper down on his jeans. He reached for her, pulling her to him and lifting her arms as he drew her top over her head and tossed it on the floor beside his shirt. Her bra came next, then his belt. She slid her hands up from his stomach, then pressed her lips to his flat, hard nipples, using her tongue to kiss him as he'd kissed her. She heard the sharp intake of his breath, then felt the bite of his fingers into the bare flesh of her shoulders.

Suddenly she was on her back again, his mouth on hers with an urgency that took her breath away. The feel of his hot damp skin against hers, the wildly incredible sensation of her breasts pressed tightly against the hard-muscled wall of his chest, sent every thought out of her mind. She needed as she'd never needed before. This man, only this man could bring her to life like this.

Slater knew he'd lost his mind, his very soul, to the woman in his arms. It had been impossible to deny himself any longer, to resist the burning ache inside him. She'd used the word *noble* to describe him only minutes ago, but there was nothing even remotely noble about the need slicing through him, nothing that even faintly resembled admirable or respectable. What he felt was as primitive, as wild, as nature itself. In that moment between insanity and reality he'd reached for her blindly. When she'd reached back, he'd known he was lost.

He ran his hands over her soft body, wishing he could touch her, kiss her, everywhere at once. He dug his hands into her hair and pulled her head backward, exposing her lovely long neck to him, kissing the lobe of her ear, the sensitive hollow at the base of her throat. Every soft sigh, every small sound of need she uttered, drove him closer to the edge. An edge he'd struggled so hard to stay away from, an edge where control was nonexistent, where there was no reason, no thought, only feelings. Feelings he'd thought himself incapable of, feelings that went much deeper than the physical.

She called to him then, murmuring his name as she tugged at the denim around his hips. He rose over her, shoving the jeans down and away, then hooked his thumbs in the splash of lace across her hips and slid her panties away, leaving only her skirt. Impatient, he left the cotton fabric bunched around her waist and moved between her thighs, stroking the moist heat of her body with the pad of his thumb. She surged upward at the contact, biting her bottom lip as she gasped, then pleaded. The sight of her flushed, naked body opening to him, writhing under his intimate caress finally drove him over the edge. Lowering himself to her, he eased her thighs apart with his hands, then slid into her slowly, with a restraint that brought sweat to his brow.

He held her gaze, watching her green eyes darken with passion. She reached for him, pulling him closer to her, arching her body upward to hurry his progress and deepen the contact. The tight, moist sheath of her body closed around him with a pleasure somewhere between ecstasy and pain. She wrapped her legs around him, her silky limbs drawing him closer still. Deeper. Her hair spilled across the pillow under her head, and her lips, parted and swollen from his kisses, breathed his name.

And when he'd slid into her body, completely, wholly, he stared down at her. Eyelids heavy with desire, eyes smoky green, she stared back. "Yes," she whispered, cupping his face in her hands and pressing her lips lightly to his.

Raw, primitive need swept through him like a firestorm. Jaw clenched tight, heart pounding furiously, he began to move, his rhythm building slowly, urgently, powerfully. Her fingernails dug into his shoulders, his hands tangled in her hair. Gasping with pleasure, she answered him thrust for thrust, tightening around him, bringing him closer to the release his body so desperately craved.

Surging upward, she cried out suddenly, closing her eyes as she twisted her head to the side. She shuddered, again and again, and the wave of her climax crashed into him. Groaning tightly, he plunged deeper, pressing her farther into the bed, then farther still, nearly crushing her with the violent force of his release.

His breath ragged, he buried his face in her neck and gathered her gently in his arms, her name a whisper on his lips.

The late-afternoon sun poured through the open bedroom window in ethereal streaks of brilliant white light. A breeze lifted the lace edges of the curtains, carrying with it the sweet scent of roses, and outside, in the tall elm beside the house, sparrows fussed nosily over their nests.

Time had become nonexistent for Kasey. Her senses had slowly returned, and she became increasingly aware of the man draped over her. Their breathing had slowed, and the fine sheen of perspiration covering their bodies had begun to cool.

She wanted desperately to speak, to say something, but she had no words. What words could there possibly be that would express what she felt? And if there were, would he want to hear them? Would he want to know that she'd never felt like this before, that she'd never even thought such exquisite pleasure possible?

He started to move away from her, but she linked her leg over his and circled her arms around his neck.

"I'll break you," he said huskily.

"If I broke that easily," she said seductively, "I'd already be in a thousand pieces."

His brow furrowed. "I hurt you, didn't I? Dammit, I'm sorry, I just lost control and I—"

She pulled his mouth to hers, cutting off his apology. "Don't you dare tell me you're sorry, not for anything," she murmured against his lips. "So help me, I'll throw you out this bedroom window if you do."

He smiled at the image. "That oughta set the town tongues wagging even faster. Hugh Slater thrown naked from Kasey Donovan's second-story bedroom."

Her soft laugh turned to a low moan as he parted her lips with his tongue. His kiss was long and deep, a slow, sensuous exploration that left her light-headed. She slid her hands down his back, over the sinewy planes and valleys, then farther down, over solid muscle that flexed instinctively when she touched him, bringing him deeper inside her. The sound he made had an animal quality to it, almost a growl of pleasure. He tightened his hold on her, and she gasped as he rolled unexpectedly onto his back, bringing her with him without breaking contact.

"Smooth move." Kasey raised herself and made lazy circles on his chest with one daring finger. She could hear the purr in her husky voice. "Almost as impressive as the quarter trick."

He lifted his brows. "Almost, huh? You're a hard lady to please, Acacia."

"Which means you should be very proud of yourself," she said, sliding her finger down over the smooth skin of his belly, "because you're looking at one very pleased lady."

He chuckled, then turned his attention elsewhere, skimming his hands up her sleek thighs to where their bodies were still joined. Electricity danced along skin as he moved over her bottom, then slid slowly up her stomach. Her breath caught when he hesitated, then, ever so slightly, he brushed his knuckles on the soft underside of her breasts.

His eyes narrowed as he looked at her, and his expression grew darkly sensual. She would have thought she'd be embarrassed; making love while it was still light outside, having him look at her naked body as if he wanted to consume her. But she wasn't. Nothing could have felt more natural to her, more exciting and wonderful. She loved him. She'd always loved him. She always would love him.

But there was no always for them. There was only now. She refused to think about tonight or tomorrow. She would have this time, however long it would be, and she would cherish it.

Gently, as if he had all the time in the world, he traced the underswell of her breast, then slid his thumbs upward to caress the tight buds of her nipples. She caught her lip and let her head fall back in submission to his erotic touch. The heat began to build again, and she felt him harden inside her. He covered her breasts with his rough palms, rubbing her sensitive skin until she gasped at the exquisite pleasure. She heard his breathing grow ragged, matching hers, felt him begin to move under her. She moved, too, feeling as if she'd been turned inside out, with every nerve exposed. His hands kneaded and stroked, his hips surged upward.

Every muscle in her body tightened and she moaned at the tension spiraling inside her. He moved inside her, filling her as she'd never been filled, loving her as she'd never been loved. He took hold of her hips then, guiding her, steadying her, and she braced herself on his arms, moving in the rhythm set from ancient times. She felt a sense of power she'd never experienced before and she reveled in it, giving him what he asked for and more.

The pleasure increased, coiling inside her, and he thrust wildly, his hands gripping her hips like a vise. He closed his eyes on a grimace, and his groan was deep and hoarse as he shuddered uncontrollably. With a sharp cry, she followed, then collapsed onto his chest, certain she would never move again.

Eight

She woke slowly to pale moonlight and the scent of roses. It took a moment to realize where she was, then another moment to decide if she was dreaming. The bed lay empty and cold beside her, but judging from the condition of the tousled sheets, and the state of her undress, making love with Slater hadn't been a dream, after all.

Well, not in the literal sense, anyway, she thought with a slow smile.

Her stomach growled, and she rose on one elbow and looked at the bedside clock. Nine o'clock. Good heavens! No wonder she was hungry. They'd had hamburgers in town for lunch, but dinner had completely slipped by unnoticed.

Sitting, she stretched her arms out with a satisfied yawn, then pulled the sheet up to cover herself. What a sight she must be. The little makeup she'd had on would certainly be gone, and her hair must look like she'd styled it with a hand mixer. She combed her fingers through the tangled mess, trying to bring it to some kind of order, and noticed her clothes on the floor beside the bed. She couldn't help the rush of heat that flooded her insides. When she noticed that Slater's clothes were gone, her fingers stilled.

She listened for any sounds from downstairs, but there was only silence. She slammed her eyes shut and drew in a breath, feeling as if her heart had dropped into her stomach.

She'd promised herself that no matter what happened, there would be no regret. Not for the past week they'd spent together, and certainly not for this afternoon—and evening—in each other's arms. Every day they'd had together had been a gift, and she refused to be sorry for even one minute of it.

Breath held, she listened.

Still nothing.

He wouldn't have just left, she thought, biting her bottom lip. Not without telling her, not without saying goodbye. She sat on the edge of the bed and was reaching for her blouse when the smell of something wonderful floated to her.

Food.

She glanced toward the open bedroom door and saw his silhouette there in the darkness, filling the door and filling her senses. Relief poured through her.

"Kasey, you awake?" he whispered.

Ignoring the flutter in her stomach, she leaned back in the bed and pulled the sheet up to cover herself. "Only if you've brought me some of whatever smells so incredibly good."

He chuckled softly, then she felt the mattress dip as he sat beside her and turned on the bedside lamp. Her heart skipped at the sight of his bare chest underneath his un-buttoned shirt, then her stomach rumbled at the sight of the heaping plate of grilled ham and cheese sandwiches and chocolate chip cookies he set on the nightstand.

"Ah, gourmet dining." She forced her attention away from the unsnapped button of his jeans, then grabbed a triangle of sandwich and groaned with pleasure as she tasted the first bite.

"And here I thought you'd be happy to see me." He picked up a half sandwich. "You're just thinking of your stomach."

"I had a few other things on my mind," she murmured breathlessly.

"Oh?" He took a big bite of his sandwich, then smiled with male satisfaction. "Like what?"

"Well—" she nibbled thoughtfully and swallowed "—I've got to feed the horses, and of course I can't help but wonder if the boys are all right. The refrigerator could definitely use a good going through and then—"

She wouldn't have thought a man so large could move so quickly. He threw his sandwich back on the plate, then pulled her underneath him as he covered her mouth with his. She tasted the warm, melted cheese on his lips and the salty flavor of the ham. Tossing her own sandwich back on the plate, she curled her arms around his neck and pulled him closer.

"I already fed the horses," he said roughly. "The boys are having a great time, and I was just in the refrigerator. It's fine. Now try again."

She brushed her mouth against his, then traced the out-line of his lips with her tongue. "I was thinking about you," she breathed. "About the way you make me feel."

"How do I make you feel?" He slanted his mouth and rubbed his lips lightly against hers.

"Good," she whispered, arching her body upward, irritated that a sheet and his clothes separated their bodies. "Wonderful. Fantastic. Is that enough for your male ego?"

"I'm afraid not," he said with almost desperation in his voice as he tugged the sheet away. "Not nearly enough."

He made love to her slowly this time, taking her to the edge with his touch, then pulling back to heighten the sensations. Again and again, until he was as naked as she was, as wild. And when she wrapped herself around him and gave herself up to the intense pleasure spiraling through her, he was with her. Every breath, every touch, every heartbeat.

He woke to sunlight and the smell of bacon frying. Face in his pillow and a smile on his lips, he pulled the wonderful aroma into his lungs. The incredible contentment permeating his entire body and the warmth of the sun on his back lured him deeper into his pillow.

The sun on his back?

Cursing, he swung his legs out of bed and looked at the bedside clock. Nine o'clock! He swore again and reached for his jeans. He never overslept. Old habits and natural body rhythms had never let him sleep in.

But then, old habits and body rhythms had never spent the night with a woman like Kasey before.

In fact, he realized with a frown, he'd never spent the night with *any* woman before.

He tugged his jeans on, then sat on the edge of the bed and reached for his socks and boots. It certainly wasn't that he'd been a saint for the past ten years. He'd pulled his boots off in more than one woman's bedroom. He'd simply never stayed until morning. So there'd be no misunderstandings, no misconceptions about a relationship. He'd kept his life simple that way.

Until now.

He sighed and closed his eyes. There was no simple when it came to Kasey. Not from the moment he'd read that damn ad. Not then, not now.

God. He dragged his hands through his hair. Certainly not now.

He riffled through his duffel bag and came up with a gray T-shirt, then made his way down the stairs as he pulled it on. He heard her in the kitchen, singing along with the radio. He paused, then took a deep breath and went into the kitchen.

She stood at the stove, her back to him, and he couldn't help but smile as he watched her scooping potatoes onto a plate, singing along with Tricia Yearwood about being ''in love with the boy.'' He also couldn't help but notice the sexy swing of her hips as she moved with the tune. Slender hips that fit his body like no other woman's ever had before, hips that he'd held only a short while ago.

The image of those hips against his, the memory of her soft curves and silky skin underneath him, made his blood heat up instantly. He wanted her again. Now. Yesterday and last night hadn't been enough. He would leave wanting her as badly as he had before they'd made love.

No, he realized, with a mixture of anger and despair. He'd leave wanting her more. More than he would have ever dreamed possible.

Kasey knew that Slater was standing in the doorway watching her. She gave him the minute she knew he needed to fortify himself for what she expected would be his ''morning after'' speech. A speech, she thought with a twinge in her heart, that he'd given countless times. She had no idea how the other women dealt with it, but she knew she wanted to rail like a crazy woman and wail like a baby.

Calmly, purposefully, she took her time as she filled two plates with eggs, bacon and potatoes, then turned to face him. "Morning."

He nodded, his gaze intense as he watched her set the plates on the table beside two cups of steaming coffee. She prayed he couldn't see the way her hands were shaking.

"I've got to go feed the horses," he said blandly.

She rolled her eyes and shook her head. "Slater, I've fed them. Just like I fed them every day before you showed up. Just like I'll feed them every day after you've left. Now sit down and eat."

He hesitated, then sat at the table, his face grim. "Kasey, I—"

"I'm really sorry about last night," she cut him off as she sat at the table beside him. "I mean, I have no idea whatever came over me, taking advantage of you like I did. I never should have let it get out of hand like that. Obviously I just wasn't thinking clearly. I mean, it was great and all, but I don't want you to get the wrong idea, you know, about you and me. Your friendship means a lot to me, and I wouldn't want to risk that for anything."

Stunned, he simply stared at her, his brow tightly knotted between his dark eyes.

She took a bite of bacon and smiled sweetly. "How'm I doin' so far?"

"This is serious, Kase," he said evenly. "Don't make light of it."

"And what would you have me make of it, Slate?" She leaned back in her chair with a sigh. "Would you prefer tears? Or maybe just pretend nothing happened between us at all? Or better yet, how about we just have

a nice laugh at our stupidity, punch each other in the arm
and send Christmas cards each year?''

His eyes narrowed, and she could have sworn she saw
a muscle jump in his jaw. "I don't know what I want.''

She lifted her brows. "Well, now, there's a good place
to start. Honesty.''

She struggled to keep her pulse from racing when he
reached for her hand and pulled her onto his lap.
"Kase—'' he laced his fingers with hers ''—nothing like
that—like you—has ever happened to me.''

She could handle his temper, his foolishness. What she
couldn't handle was his tenderness. Her throat felt thick;
her chest ached, and all she wanted to do was crawl inside him. "I take it that's a bad thing.''

"Yes, I mean, no…ah, hell, Kasey.'' He rolled his
head back and sighed. "I've got a job waiting for me.
That's my life now. What I do, who I am. I don't know
anything else anymore. Horses and kids and camping
trips are foreign territory to me.''

Was he trying to convince her? she wondered. Or himself? Either way, the outcome would be the same: he was
leaving. She wouldn't beg him to stay, she wouldn't even
ask. If he did stay, it had to be because he wanted to,
because he needed to. Because he needed her.

But she knew that would never happen. He'd spent ten
years making sure he needed no one, and that no one
needed him. One night wasn't about to change that, and
it was fantasy for her to think any other way.

Ignoring the tight knot forming in her stomach, she
pulled her fingers from his, then cupped his face in her
hands. "One hour or one week,'' she said softly. "Why
don't we just enjoy whatever time we have?''

His gaze met hers, and she could see the struggle in
his deep brown eyes. When her lips touched his, she felt

his rush of breath, heard the deep groan in his throat. And then he was kissing her back with a desperation that took her breath away. His hand moved up her spine, pulling her closer to him as he deepened the kiss. She trembled in his arms, leaning into him as he slanted his mouth against hers again and again.

"Slater," she murmured against his lips as she fanned her hands over his chest. "There's something I've been wanting to ask you."

He moved over her jaw and throat, his mouth greedy and open as he nibbled just below her ear. The stubble of his beard sent erotic shocks of pleasure dancing over her skin. "Hmm?"

"Did you really play the bass drum in high school?"

He hesitated, then chuckled deeply. His lips skimmed over her, tasting, exploring every sensitive dip and curve of her neck. "The principal made the entire football team choose a fine art or music class. It was either ceramics or the bass drum. At least with the drum I got to pound on something."

She laughed softly, then sucked in a breath as his tongue swept over her earlobe. "And what about *Robinson Crusoe?*"

"What about him?" he muttered, busy with her ear.

"Did you—" She bit her lower lip when he moved down her neck, blazing hot, wet kisses. "Read it ten times?"

"Hell, no," he said hoarsely, then leaned back in his chair and cradled her in his lap. "I swiped a couple of cigarettes from my dad, and Andy Johnson and I were smoking behind the toolshed. I just brought a report book with me so it would look like I was out doing homework, but that fool Johnson dropped a lit match on the open pages and they went up like dried leaves. It was either keep checking it out, or have my dad find out I'd not only burned a book, but I'd been smoking. MaryAnn doesn't know it, but she saved my butt when she finally gave it to me.''

Kasey clucked her tongue and gave his nose a tap with her finger. ''Shame on you, Hugh Slater. Stealing cigarettes and smoking at that age.''

He lifted his brows and stared down his nose at her. ''I seem to recall a certain incident with a bottle of beer in the barn.''

''I knew I should have left out that part of the story,'' she said with a grimace, then sighed and traced the outline of his lips with her fingertip. ''I'm not looking forward to all that with Cody and Troy.''

''Cody and Troy?'' Slater's expression was mock surprise. ''Those two angels? They'll never give you a snippet of trouble. Why, I see them headed for priesthood.''

Her laugh was dry and short. ''Exactly what everyone in Granite Ridge said about Hugh Slater.''

It was impossible to stop the skip of her pulse when he nipped at her finger. He took her hand in his and stared at it, his expression suddenly thoughtful. ''It's not easy being a single parent these days,'' he said quietly. ''I admire you, Kase.''

His words sent a flutter of warmth through her. ''Thanks, Slate.'' She pressed a kiss to the tip of his nose. ''But you know, it's always been difficult to be a single parent, even twenty years ago, and especially for a man.''

She felt his body go still underneath her, then felt the tension tighten his muscles. His lips were pressed firmly together as he met her steady gaze. ''Why have you suddenly become my father's champion?''

Sighing, she smoothed her hands over the neck of his T-shirt. ''There was something in his eyes yesterday when he looked at you. He was hurting, Slater. It was there only for a moment, but it was there.''

"A person has to be able to feel in order to hurt," Slater said dryly.

She shook her head slowly. "Everyone has feelings. Some people just hide them better than others, because it hurts too much to acknowledge them. Because they're afraid to let themselves feel. Did you know he had an operation three years ago?''

His gaze snapped back to hers, but he said nothing.

"I didn't think so. A horse trampled him, broke his leg in three places and nearly crushed his skull. He nearly died on the way to the hospital in Abilene.''

"It would take more than a horse to kill my father," Slater said flatly, but Kasey saw the hard thin line of his mouth and the imperceptible narrowing of his left eye.

He slid her off his lap as he rose, then he walked to the kitchen window and looked out, his shoulders tight and his back straight.

If stubborn were land, she thought, then Jack and Hugh Slater would own all of Texas.

"Brian's father was the surgeon," she went on casually, retrieving the coffeepot and warming Slater's cooling cup. "The way I hear it, he literally saved your father's life and his leg.''

"I'll send him a fruit basket." Slater folded his arms and turned sharply to face her. "Look, Kasey, if you're expecting me to forget a lifetime of indifference from my father and suddenly feel sorry for the man because he had an accident, then you're saddling the wrong horse.''

"I'm not expecting anything from you, Slater.'' Kasey's voice was as cool as the food on their plates. "I just think before you leave you might talk to him, that's all. Ten years is a long time.''

"I told you, I didn't come here to see my father."

"Well, you probably didn't come here to crawl under the sheets with me, either. But that little change of plans didn't turn out to be so bad, did it?"

An anger close to rage narrowed his eyes and he struggled to hold on to his control. She was trying to make him lose his temper, he realized. To prove that he did care. Well, he wasn't going to fight with Kasey, certainly not over his father. "Are you actually comparing what happened between us with my father?"

"It's not so different. You fought against what you were feeling for me, just like you're fighting your feelings for your father." Her touch on his arm was gentle. "It's not too late, Slater. It's never too late."

"It is for Jeanie," he said tightly.

She sighed and leaned her head against his shoulder. "Your father wasn't driving the car that killed Jeanie any more than you were. Her death was just as hard on him as it was you. But the loss of a child—and a wife—is so profound, so deeply painful, that the only way to deal with it is not to deal with it. Sometimes that comes across as indifference."

He felt the jerk of a muscle in his jaw and the heat of simmering impatience. "You just don't quit, do you?"

She shook her head slowly. "Not when it's important."

"Why, Kasey? Why should this be important to you?"

She moved in front of him, slipped her fingers under his tightly folded arms. "Because you're important to me," she said softly. "Because I care about you."

He looked down at her, into her smoking green eyes, and felt as if he were drowning there, as if the very air were being sucked from him. He didn't want her to care. No more than he wanted to care. And he sure as hell didn't want to be important to her any more than he wanted her to be important to him.

Her hands on his arm, though smooth and tender, were like a cinch tightening around his chest. He didn't want this, not from her, and he fought it the only way he knew how. With anger. The heat of it coiled inside him like a serpent, then slithered to the surface.

"Even if I did talk to my father," he said coldly, "I'm not staying, Kasey."

He regretted the words the second they were out. Hurt flashed in her eyes, then a glittering moisture. She dropped her hands from him and stepped away, holding her gaze level with his.

"Is that what you think all this is?" she asked with deadly softness. "That I'm so needy, so lonely, so desperate for a man that I'd want you to reconcile with your father so you'd stay here? And me, being so conniving and all, that's probably why I went to bed with you."

God, he was an idiot. A complete, first-class, number-one idiot. "Dammit, Kasey." He softened his voice and took a step toward her. "That isn't what I meant and you know it."

She moved away from him. "I know exactly what you meant, Slater. Probably better than you know yourself."

He was moving toward her again, consumed with a mixture of anger and guilt and frustration, when the doorbell rang.

Without so much as a glance at him, she marched out of the kitchen with him right on her heels and threw open the front door. "What is it?" she barked.

Looking utterly confused, the Hackett brothers, Bobby and Billy, stood on her front porch, or rather, they filled her front porch. Though not quite as tall as Slater, they were built like steamrollers, with barrel chests and arms the diameter of telephone poles. Dressed in torn sweat-pants and cut-off T-shirts with sports slogans, they looked at Kasey sheepishly and touched the brims of their baseball caps. "How do, Kase."

"I'm sorry, guys," she said awkwardly, "but this really isn't a good time for me right now. Maybe you could come back—"

"We, uh—" Bobby scratched at his neck. "Well, we didn't exactly come to see you."

Billy grinned wide when Slater moved behind Kasey. "Hey, Slater boy. We heard y'all was in town and we come to bring you out and throw a few passes. Nobody ever had an arm like old Slater."

"Look, guys," Slater said, shoving his hands into his pockets, "I appreciate it, but—"

"Take him." Kasey had the front screen open and all but shoved him out onto the porch, then slammed the front door.

Bobby and Billy looked at each other, then Slater.

"Everything okay?" Bobby asked.

Eyes narrowed, Slater stared at the door. It was either kick it or go with the Hacketts and release a little pent-up aggression.

"Everything's just fine," he snapped. "Let's go play some ball."

Kasey heard Billy Hackett's truck drive up long after dark. She hadn't worried that Slater hadn't come back earlier, but she couldn't help her disappointment that what little time they had together had been cut into by a game of football and the Hackett brothers. Of course, she'd been the one to insist he go, but that still didn't mean she had to like it.

So playtime was over now, she thought irritably, and

the boys were back, hollering and laughing, exchanging male insults outside in her driveway. Pressing her lips tightly together, she forced her concentration back to the jigsaw puzzle she'd set up on the coffee table in the living room, determined not to go outside and show even the slightest interest that he was home.

The whooping and yelling continued for several minutes, then Billy's truck skidded away, blasting its horn all the way up her drive. At the sound of heavy boot steps on the front porch, Kasey hunched intently over her puzzle, searching for the centerpiece of a sunflower.

"Kasey!" He threw open the door and propelled himself into the entryway, catching his boot on the braided rug and stumbling several feet before he caught himself. "Kasey, where are you, honey?"

He caught sight of her in the living room and wobbled toward her. Dropping to his knees, he slipped an arm around her shoulders. "Hey, darling, whatcha doing there?"

He was drunk as the proverbial skunk.

His jeans were torn at the knees and covered with grass stains, his T-shirt ripped at the shoulder and spotted with blood—his own, she assumed, based on the cut over his left eye. He reeked of beer and sweat and dirt.

She should be mad at him, dammit, she wanted to be, but his inebriated expression was one of childlike innocence.

Shaking her head, she tolerated the wet smack he gave her straight on the lips, then linked her arm around his waist and helped him stand. "Come on, tiger, let's get you upstairs."

"I was gonna help with the puzzle," he complained.

"Later." The man couldn't find his own hand right now, let alone fit together pieces in a jigsaw puzzle. She pulled him toward the stairs, fully realizing the weight of his solid muscle as she helped him up each step. He snuggled close to her, muttering endearments all the way into the bedroom, where he attempted to guide her to the bed. She had to laugh at the absurdity of his endeavor, and promised him they'd be there soon, right after he took a shower.

Fully clothed, he staggered into the tub. She waited until his T-shirt was half off before she turned the water on.

The cold water.

He gave a yelp, tangling himself in his torn T-shirt as he fell to his knees, unable to find his footing in the wet tub. The water plastered his clothes and hair to him and he swore with a fierce passion.

She let him struggle and vent for a minute, then shut the water off and stood outside the tub, arms folded. He moved with a dull slowness, practically ripping the T-shirt off himself, then lifted his glassy eyes and stared at her.

"What the hell'd you do that for?" he slurred. Water dripped from his hair down his face and onto his now-bare chest.

If only she had a camera in her hands. This was definitely a Kodak moment. "Do what?" she asked sweetly.

He combed his sopping hair away from his face, swore again, then sank back down in the tub and closed his eyes with a heavy sigh. She'd almost thought he'd passed out, but he opened his eyes after a long moment and stared up at her.

"I'm sorry, Kase," he murmured. "God, I'm sorry."

The pain she heard in his voice and saw in his dark gaze melted the last of the anger and frustration that had been simmering in her all day.

"What are you sorry for?" she asked, not certain she wanted to hear the answer, but needing to.

"I've hurt you. I didn't want to. I wanted to help you, make it right somehow."

"Make what right, Slate?"

"Jeanie," he whispered. "I let her down, too."

His soft confession was like a knife in her heart. She swallowed back the thickness in her throat and crawled into the tub with him, wrapping her arms around his cold, wet body. "No, Slater. You didn't let her down. She made her own choices. There was nothing you could do."

"She needed me," he said hoarsely. "And I was helpless. Do you know what that feels like, Kase? What it makes me feel like?"

There was agony in his voice, a dark, heavy grief that surfaced like a demon released from its chains. She pressed her cheek to his shaking chest and held him close. "I loved her, too, Slater."

His arms came around her in a crushing, painful grip that took her breath away. As if he were afraid she might leave. "You're one hell of a woman, Kasey Donovan," he murmured after several minutes, then sighed deeply, his arms relaxing as he drifted off.

"Thank you," she whispered back, and touched her lips to his. Eyes closed, he smiled.

Then snored.

With a sigh of exasperation, she stared at him, wondering not only how she was ever going to live without this man, but how she was going to get a six-foot-five, two-hundred-twenty-pound man from a bathtub into her bed.

Nine

Slater had always been told that intelligence had its limits, but stupidity knew no bounds. As he cracked open one eye and groaned at the fierce white-hot light burning his pupils, he knew that he was a living testimony to the proverb.

It took three tries before he managed a sitting position, and the pitch in his stomach nearly had him lying down again. His head threatened to roll off, and his swollen tongue stuck to the roof of his dust-dry mouth.

Somewhere between a stagger and a crawl, he managed to get himself to the bathroom. A hideous, pain-twisted creature with an ugly gash over its right eye stared back from the mirror. A face that would make children scream and old ladies faint dead away.

Because it was impossible to move with any sense of dignity, he wobbled to the shower and slid his sweatpants off, grimacing at the pain that shot through his chest.

Broken ribs, he decided, certain that nearly every bone in his body was either fractured or bruised. He was too damn old to handle a flying tackle from Bobby Hackett, and too damn old to drink the afternoon and half the night away at Weber's Bar.

He dragged his hands over his scalp, struggling to remember how he'd gotten home and into bed. There were slices of memory that involved Kasey and a jigsaw puzzle, but concentration only deepened the pounding in his head. He was in one piece—sort of—and he decided that was all he needed to know for now.

He was reaching for the shower faucet when thunder shook the house and high-pitched screaming cracked his skull into tiny pieces.

"Slater! We're home!"

Gritting his teeth—which also ached—he'd barely time to cover himself with a towel before two mini-torpedoes screeched to a halt at the bathroom.

Oblivious to his distress, and his near nakedness, Cody and Troy chattered at warp speed, both at the same time. Between the sharp pains bouncing off the inside of his skull, Slater caught bits and pieces of the boys' excitement over their camping trip.

"So will you, Slater, will you, please, please?"

He squinted, trying to put a few words together and come up with what they were asking, but a full sentence wouldn't form. Whatever it was they wanted couldn't be worse than the pain they were putting him through at the moment, so he simply waved a hand in agreement, then ushered them out the door.

Breathing a long sigh of relief, he stepped gingerly under the piercing hot needles of water and was suddenly struck by an image of himself, looking down into Kasey's eyes, right here in this very tub.

He submerged his head under the showerhead, struggling to bring the image to focus, but all he could remember was her taking off his clothes. That picture definitely brought a smile to his face, and he decided they must not be fighting anymore.

Afraid he might cut his own throat, he elected not to shave, and dressed slowly, proud that he managed all by himself, though the boots had gone on backward the first time. He smelled coffee wafting upstairs from the kitchen, and he made his way steadily toward the blissful smell like a salmon working its way upstream, knowing that heaven waited for him at the end of the long, arduous journey.

He sank into a kitchen chair, head in his hands, and mumbled what he hoped was a coherent greeting. A cup of steaming black coffee appeared under his nose, and the angel who supplied it sat in the chair across from him.

"Bless you," he managed, and slurped loudly.

"How about some buttered biscuits dripping with thick, lumpy chicken gravy?" she asked sweetly.

His stomach lurched, and though it hurt his eyeballs to do so, he stared at her over the rim of his coffee cup. "How 'bout some bamboo splinters under my fingernails while you're at it?"

She smiled innocently, then pushed a plate across the table at him. "Maybe just some dry toast, then."

He sniffed at it, and when his insides didn't turn over, he ventured a bite, then washed it down—along with two aspirins that miraculously appeared—with another swig of coffee.

He just might live after all, he decided, and even managed a thank-you when Kasey refilled his coffee cup.

"You want to fill me in on any details from last night?" he asked casually.

"Well, let's see—" she tapped at her cheek "—I cleaned out the refrigerator and found a plastic container behind the egg holder just loaded with fuzzy green mold, then I was putting some laundry away in the boys' room and found a rotting banana peel under Cody's bed. Good Lord, the smell was enough to make me pass out, and then—"

"Enough." His toast tasted like sawdust, but at least it stayed down. If she kept up her report on spoiled food, he'd be heading for the bathroom. "Whatever I did, or said, I humbly apologize."

"Not necessary," she said cheerfully. "From the looks of you, I'd say you've suffered enough."

"Gee, thanks." He scrubbed a hand over his face, then winced at the sharp pain over his right eye. "You didn't happen to tie me to the back of the truck and drag me around last night, did you?"

"So you don't remember?"

The coffee mug was halfway to his mouth when he froze. "Remember what?"

"Well, I guess under the circumstances, any woman would do." She sighed heavily, then got up from the table and filled the sink with water, squirting dish soap under the running faucet, looking terribly hurt.

"Under what circumstances?" He rose quickly, swore, and when the room stopped moving, followed her to the sink. "And what the hell kind of comment is that, 'any woman would do'?"

She sank her arms elbow high into bubbles and circled a pot with a sponge. "Well, you were rather, shall we say, impetuous."

"Are you trying to tell me that I—I mean, we—in my condition, that we, uh, slept together?"

She lifted one corner of her mouth in a provocative smile. "We took a shower together first."

That part he almost remembered. But not quite. He narrowed his eyes, forcing the dullness from his brain.

And then he did remember. He was half dressed; she was fully clothed. Cold water. That he remembered only too well. He moved behind her, wrapping his arms around her waist and pulling her close.

"Ah, yes, I do remember now." He heard her sharp intake of breath as he stroked her stomach with his thumbs. "You were amazing, Kase."

She glanced over her shoulder at him. "I was?"

"Absolutely awesome."

"Really."

She tried to pull away from him, but he held her close against him. In spite of himself, his aching bones and splitting head, he felt his body respond to her round, firm bottom pressed against him.

"In fact," he murmured against her neck, "I think we should do it again, right here. Right now."

He flipped the cold water on before she could move and held his hand under the faucet, spraying water all over the front of her. She screamed and twisted away from him, throwing an armful of bubbles at him, catching him in the chest and face. He held on to her arm and scooped handful after handful of bubbles and water on her, until wet and laughing, they both went down on the floor.

They were still tossing bubbles back and forth when Cody and Troy were suddenly standing over them, fishing poles in hand. The boys looked at each other and shook their heads.

''We're ready,'' Cody chirped loudly.

''Ready for what?'' Slater asked, certain he wasn't going to like the answer.

''Did you forget?'' Kasey sat up, and his angel had a devil of a smile on her face. ''You promised to take the boys fishing.''

''Brian's dad says that fishing is really good in Alaska,'' Cody said, and Troy nodded, his mouth full of shredded baseball chewing gum. ''Maybe we can come see you sometime and go fishing together. Brian's dad says that they have salmon there big as a boat.''

Slater lay stretched out on the bank of the creek, one hand tucked under his head, the other holding a fishing pole. His Stetson covered his face, but the warmth of the afternoon sun seeped through his T-shirt and jeans, easing the aches he'd thought certain he'd die of only two hours ago. And the stomach he'd thought would never hold another bite grumbled for one of the sandwiches that Kasey had packed along with cookies, chips and fruit. They'd gobbled up the cookies as soon as they cast their first line, the chips about thirty minutes later, and the sandwiches were finally calling out to be eaten.

He sat and tipped his hat back, half listening to Cody babble on, half fantasizing about a curvy redhead whom these boys happened to call Mom. The creek was running shallow right now and no one had actually caught anything yet, but the boys didn't seem to care. They'd gone on their first camping trip and had a taste of fishing, and now they were as hooked as the trout Brian's dad had caught yesterday at the lake. They were certain a monster catch awaited them, which was what the guy at the bait shop had told the youngsters when they'd bought worms earlier.

Worm Boy. Slater remembered what MaryAnn had called the bait shop owner. Slater narrowed his eyes as he also remembered that Worm Boy had asked about Kasey, not casually, but with interest—male interest.

Slater's hands tightened on the fishing pole. He hadn't liked the look in the guy's eye when he said Kasey's name.

He didn't like it one little bit.

And yesterday, he recalled, hadn't Bobby *and* Billy asked about Kasey, too? He'd shrugged it off at the time, but now, as he remembered, they'd both had that same look in their eye.

He scowled at his fishing line, wondering if the wolves would all be moving in for the kill once he left. She was a big girl, of course, and she could certainly handle the likes of Worm Boy and the Hacketts. He couldn't imagine for a minute—a second—that Kasey would give those guys a second look. They were all wrong for her. Besides, she'd told him several times now she didn't want a husband.

He pressed his lips tightly together. But that didn't mean she didn't want a man. Lord knew the woman had more passion, more fire in her than any woman he'd ever met. That passion and those fires would need tending to, he realized irritably.

Cody was still chatting on about Brian's dad, and it struck Slater that it wasn't just Kasey that would need a man. Her sons were hungry for a father, a male figure to coach their Little League games and shoot hoops with them. Someone they could learn from and look up to, someone who knew how to be soft when they were hurting and firm when they were full of the devil. Someone who knew how to be a good father, who could love them as if they were his own sons.

But that someone could never be him. He wished it could. Damn, he wished it could. But Kasey and her sons deserved a hell of a lot more than he could ever give them. He'd never been able to stay in one place for long and even now, after these few short days he'd spent here, he'd begun to feel restless. Uneasy. As if the walls were closing slowly in on him. The need to move on had grown stronger every day until there was nothing else for him to do but leave. It had nothing to do with Kasey and the boys, it was just him, who he was.

"Slater! I caught one, I caught one!" Troy jumped up and tugged on the taut fishing line. Cody jumped up, too, hollering encouragement to his little brother.

His own reflections forgotten, Slater threw his pole down and moved behind Troy, helping him reel the line. A small but nonetheless determined trout wiggled furiously as they pulled it out of the water. Troy and Cody watched with barely contained excitement as Slater freed the fish from the hook and dropped it into a bucket filled with water.

"Nice job, Troy." Slater grinned down at the boy and ruffled his hair.

Smiling wide, Troy looked up at him, then unexpectedly threw his arms around his legs and hugged him. Stunned, Slater simply stared for a long moment, then swallowed the thickness in his throat, knelt, and hugged him back.

The mare tossed up her head with a loud whinny, then broke into a gallop, her fiery mane and tail flying, her nostrils flared and nose pressed to the wind. Sleek, solid muscles flexed and tightened while her hooves pounded the soft, sandy dirt of the corral. Overhead the sky was deep, deep blue and the scent of horse and dust and leather permeated the warm afternoon air.

With a sense of abandon, Kasey held the end of the lead line and turned with each pass Miss Lucy made, her own hair sailing wildly over her shoulders. How she'd missed all this, working with animals, the open expanse of land, a house to call her own. Ranching was hard work, but it was a labor of love, of commitment. A sense of home and devotion and responsibility.

All the things that scared the hell out of Slater.

She couldn't shake the sight of him walking to the truck this morning with her sons, fishing poles in hand and brown paper bags filled with food she'd packed. The sight of Cody's and Troy's excited faces as they'd driven off, the sight of three hands, one big, two small, waving at her from the truck windows. She hadn't known it was possible to feel such joy and misery at the same time.

Ten days ago, everything in her life had fit as neatly into place as the pieces of that jigsaw puzzle in her living room. Independence, self-confidence, pride—she'd worked hard and earned back every piece of herself that she'd lost in the years she'd been married to Paul, then put those pieces together to make a life for herself and her sons. She'd vowed that nothing, and no one, would ever have a hold over her again.

And then Slater showed up at her front door and shot her vow—and every other piece of her life—to hell.

But she'd made it through other disappointments in her life, she thought determinedly, and she'd damn well make it through Hugh Slater, too.

Raising one gloved hand over her head, she waved a fist and hollered, not certain if she was motioning the mare on, or venting her anger.

"Hey, Kasey!"

She whipped around at the unexpected shout. A man stood on the corral fencing, waving to her. She couldn't see his face under his white cowboy hat, but he had the long, lean build of a working man and the worn denims and chambray shirt to match.

She wasn't expecting anyone, she thought almost irritably, hardly in the mood for drop-by hellos and polite conversation. Slater and the boys would be coming back soon, and she'd already planned a nice dinner and getting her sons into bed early. Not only because they'd had a busy weekend and their first day of school was tomorrow, but with Slater ready to bounce out of here like he had springs on his boots, she wanted every minute they had together to be special, with just her and the boys.

Squinting, she let loose of the lead line and pulled off her gloves as she walked over to the fence. The man looked familiar somehow, but she still hadn't made a connection.

"It's Jim Burke." He smiled with straight, even teeth and touched the brim of his hat. "I used to work for your dad about twelve years ago."

Jim Burke? She did remember him, though not well. She'd only been fifteen at the time and had such a crush on Slater, she wouldn't have noticed anyone else. Amazing how little things had changed in her life in that regard.

They shook hands and though he held her fingers in his a little longer than she would have liked, he had a firm, confident grip and a warmth in his blue eyes she couldn't help but admire.

"That's a right fine filly you got there." He nodded to Miss Lucy. "The two of you make quite a sight."

She felt the warmth of a blush at his compliment. "Thanks, I think. What can I do for you?"

"I'm here about the ad."

She felt her spine stiffen. "And which ad is that?" she asked tightly. Mr. Plucket had finally pulled the husband ad, but she'd still received a few calls and letters.

"The one in the *Granite Ridge Gazette*." His grin was crooked, his blue eyes amused. "You were looking for a stud."

"I might be." She eyed him warily. What she did remember about Jim was that he'd been quiet and kept mostly to himself, but he'd been a hard worker and a good horseman. She had no idea where he was working now, or if he even had a place of his own. "I'm still sorting through the bids I've already received."

It was an out-and-out lie. She hadn't been able to afford any of the bids she'd truly been interested in, and the ones she could afford, weren't right for Miss Lucy.

She heard the staccato blare of a horn and looked over Jim's shoulder as Slater pulled his truck alongside the corral. Troy and Cody were out of the truck and running toward her before Slater could even cut the engine.

"We caught loads of fish, Mom." Cody danced around her. "Both me and Troy. We had the best day, ever. Didn't we, Slater?"

It *had* been a good day, Slater thought, his gaze locked on the man standing beside Kasey. He'd gone to school with Jim Burke, but Jim had been one grade lower and ran with a different crowd. Slater knew that Jim had worked for Kasey's dad after he graduated high school, and he also knew that the man was good with horses. For some reason, the thought annoyed him. "Jim."

"Hey, Slater. Heard you were back." Jim leaned casually against the corral fence.

"Not back." Slater wondered what else Jim had heard, then reached into the bed of the truck and pulled several trout out of a bucket. Chests puffed out, Cody and Troy proudly displayed their catch. "Just stopping through. What brings you by?"

"Just talking shop with Kasey. Hoping we can do some business together."

Slater quickly kicked down the little green creature that popped up in his gut. He had no right to ask or stick his nose into Kasey's affairs—*business matters*—he quickly amended not liking the sound of *affair* one little bit.

"I'll leave you to talk, then," he said, glancing at Kasey, who was busy praising her sons on their expert fishing abilities. "I promised Cody and Troy a lesson on fish cleaning."

"Need some help?" Jim asked. "I've cleaned a few fish in my time."

It was an innocent offer, but it stuck in Slater's craw. He shook his head. "We can manage, thanks."

And he would have managed just fine, too. He never would have sliced one of the fish in two if he hadn't been so preoccupied with wondering what Jim and Kasey were talking about with such intensity. Nor would he have cut his finger if he hadn't seen Jim—as if he had every right—take Miss Lucy's lead line from Kasey when they'd walked back to the barn.

"That one still alive?" Troy asked when the fish Slater was cleaning flipped out of his hand for the third time.

"Just slippery," Slater mumbled, glancing at the barn at the sound of Kasey's bright laugh.

"Whatcha gonna do with all those guts?" Cody asked with all the fascination and curiosity of an eight-year-old boy.

"Bury 'em under your bedroom window." Slater dropped the last fish in the bucket. "The Native Americans believe it wards off the evil spirits."

He'd never heard such a thing, but it sounded good, and besides, it would give him a good reason to go out to the barn to get a shovel. Wouldn't hurt Kasey's roses, either.

"Spirits?" Cody asked, his eyes wide. "You mean, like ghosts?"

Damn. That's all he needed on his conscience. Two kids terrified to go to sleep because they thought evil spirits and ghosts were lurking about. "Nah, not like ghosts. And you not only keep the evil spirits away, you summon forth the good ones, as well. The ones who protect you and make good things happen. You boys rinse these fish, and I'll go get the shovel."

Proud of himself at his save, he strolled into the barn. Jim and Kasey stood next to Miss Lucy's stall. Jim had hold of the mare's head, stroking the blaze of white that ran up her nose as he fed her a carrot. Slater felt his gut tighten at the way Jim was looking at Kasey, probably thinking that he'd have the woman eating out of his hand before long, too. Neither Jim nor Kasey gave him a second glance.

Jaw clenched tight, he stalked into the tack room and snatched the shovel from behind the door, knocking a metal bucket and two bridles off their hooks, then dropping the shovel on his foot as he scrambled to catch the falling paraphernalia.

"You okay?" Kasey called out.

He swore silently—and vehemently—at the pain traveling up from his foot straight to his eyeballs. He sucked in a sharp breath and let it out. "Fine. No problem."

Composing himself, he came back into the barn, casting a nonchalant glance toward Kasey and Jim. They were involved in a quiet conversation and though he strained to hear, he couldn't understand a single word. If he'd been paying closer attention to where he was going, instead of trying to eavesdrop, he would have seen the wheelbarrow.

He went over the handles, then down on his butt. Hard.

"Slater!" Kasey hurried over and knelt beside him, her green eyes narrowed with concern. "Are you all right?"

All right? He glanced at Jim, who was looking at him with a mixture of amusement and sympathy. Hell, no, he wasn't all right. His pride had more holes at the moment than a tin can on a shooting range.

"I'm fine." He waved her off and stood, brushing the dust from his jeans. "I, uh, caught my boot in a hole, that's all."

At least everyone was too polite to mention the barn floor was perfectly smooth.

"You're bleeding." Kasey took hold of his left hand and frowned. "You cut your finger."

"It's nothing." He wasn't about to tell her he'd missed with the knife because he'd been thinking about her and Jim. Besides, he liked the way she was fussing over him.

"It's deep," she said, shaking her head. "We'd better clean this up and put something on it."

"This little scratch? I can't even feel it." It stung like hell, but he was so pleased with her attention, it was all he could do not to grin.

"Don't argue with me, Hugh Slater. Infection and gangrene are two shakes away from a cut this deep. Now get in the house and wash it thoroughly."

"Don't see what all the fuss is about." He shrugged, then stuck his healthy hand out to Jim. "Well, see you around."

"At the carnival next Saturday." Jim clasped hold of Slater's hand, then smiled as he turned to Kasey. "Heard you were signed up for the picnic basket auction, Kasey.''

''I hadn't even unloaded the moving truck before Nora Parsons from the Ladies' Auxiliary had me signed up. Got me for one shift at the milk can toss, too.''

Jim laughed. ''She got me for the rifle range.''

Hey, I'm bleeding here, folks, Slater thought irritably, hoping that someone missed on one of those rifles. Just maybe that someone would be him.

Not that he expected to be here that long, of course. He'd thought a day or two more, at best, just 'cause he wanted to see how the boys' first couple of days at school went and all.

And a couple more days with Kasey was damn appealing, too.

He was washing up when Kasey came into the bathroom upstairs and leaned against the doorjamb, her arms crossed as she watched him dry his hands. ''You want to tell me why my sons are digging a hole by my rosebushes?''

''We're fertilizing.'' He dragged the towel over his wet face.

''There's manure getting thrown around, all right.'' She moved to the toilet and set the lid down. ''Now sit.''

He did as he was told, awed at the command and authority in her voice. No woman had bothered over him like this since he was a little boy. He had a fleeting image of his mother bustling over him when he was about eight, a scraped knee, he recalled. She'd sang something to him, something silly about a monkey and elephant, then made him chocolate pudding.

''Hey!'' he yelled at the sudden flame of heat that shot up from his finger to the base of his skull. She'd sprayed some antiseptic on his cut when he wasn't looking. *"Hey!"* he yelled louder when she sprayed again.

Shaking her head, she picked up his hand and blew on his finger. "Better?"

Much. He definitely liked the gentle touch of her hand, and the soft, cooling sensation of her breath on his finger. In fact, he liked it a lot. Her lips were pursed in a small *O,* as if she were whistling, her expression intent as she studied the cut. He'd never noticed the tiny ripples of gold and brown in her green eyes before, or the faint cluster of freckles beside her left eyebrow. Her cheeks were rosy, perhaps from working with the horses, or, he liked to think, because he'd slipped an arm around her waist.

With the skill of a surgeon, she wrapped a bandage around his finger, then smiled as she examined her work. "You'll live."

"A kiss is supposed to make it all better."

She looked at him, tilting her head with skepticism. "Aren't you a little old for that?"

"Not for what I had in mind." He pulled her onto his lap, sliding his hands up her back as he bent his head and covered her surprised gasp with his mouth. Her palms pressed against his chest, neither a surrender nor a resistance, then slowly her fingers curled into his T-shirt and she leaned into him, parting her lips with a soft sigh.

His hand cradled her head as he moved his mouth over hers, consuming every sweet thrust of her tongue against his. She made a small, quiet sound deep in her throat, a whimper, and he went crazy, suddenly filled with an urgency that stunned him.

He kicked the bathroom door shut, deepening the kiss as his hand sought her breast. She arched into him as he palmed the soft flesh in his hand, then moaned when he thrust her T-shirt up and covered the thin lacy peak of her bra with his mouth, drawing her nipple to a tight hard bud through the delicate fabric. She pulled him closer to her, her breath ragged, and the movement of her bottom against him had him hard and aching.

With a long, frustrated groan, she pulled away suddenly and stood, tucking her T-shirt back into place.

She looked so damn sexy, with her face flushed and her lips still wet from his kiss, he started to reach for her again. The sound of Cody and Troy arguing over who got to cover the guts with dirt drifted in from the open bathroom window and stopped him.

That kiss had definitely not made anything better, he thought miserably. He was in a lot more pain now than he was before. But he had no one to blame but himself. "Sorry. Bad timing."

Smiling, she combed her fingers through her hair, then leaned forward and pressed a kiss to his forehead. "Hugh Slater, what am I going to do with you?"

He stood and pulled her into his arms, then whispered, in detail, several erotic suggestions that made her shudder.

And that night, after the boys went to bed and were fast asleep, he made her shudder again. And again, and again...

Ten

Saturday morning, Slater pulled the truck into the freshly raked dirt parking lot behind the Granite Ridge High School baseball field and parked between a blue minivan and a green Explorer. In front of them a huge white banner stretched across the backstop fence. Welcome To The Granite Ridge Ladies' Auxiliary Carnival And Auction.

Behind the backstop, on the baseball field, a fire-engine red Tilt-A-Whirl spun furiously, emitting human screams with each stomach-turning revolution; a three-story-high Ferris wheel towered majestically, sweeping its passengers upward, then down again, while brightly colored merry-go-round horses galloped in steady circles around twelve-foot-high carousel mirrors to the tune of "When the Saints Go Marching In." Brilliant balloons in clusters of red and blue and yellow bounced from every concession and game stand, and the scent of hot dogs and popcorn and freshly baked churros filled the warm, late morning air.

Kasey had barely opened her door before Cody and Troy scrambled over her lap and spilled out of the truck.

"Not so fast." She pulled her sons back. "We need to establish a few things first."

They were nodding compliance, but only half listening, Slater knew, as Kasey listed the forbidden: walking off by themselves, forgetting their manners and no arguing. Slater nearly laughed out loud at the no arguing. She might as well ask them not to breathe, he thought, settling his Stetson on his head, then slipping on a pair of aviator sunglasses. He was pulling Kasey's auction basket out of the bed of his truck when he heard her say, "Understand?" and the boys were off as if they'd been shot out of a cannon.

"Lord grant me patience," he heard her mutter, watching her sons race to the ticket gate.

She'd worn a pale denim dress today, with a scoop neck and a long skirt that curled around her legs, and strappy little white sandals that showed off her red painted toes. He'd watched her paint those toes last night, and just the thought of her bent over those long legs brought a tightening in his loins. And the thought of how he'd slid his hands up those smooth silky legs after the polish had dried, and the way her hips had moved under him when he'd loved her, brought that tightening in his loins to a threshold of near pain.

She turned and smiled at him then, tucking a wayward strand of wavy auburn hair behind her ear. It was an innocent gesture, but so sexy, so completely devastating to his already weakened state, he nearly dropped to his knees.

He'd never intended to stay this long, but somehow,

each day flew by, and there was some little thing or other around the ranch he wanted to take care of before he headed north.

And the nights. Lord, the nights. A woman had never turned him inside out and upside down before. He felt alive with her, aware of life like he'd never been before. It was exhilarating, arousing...

Terrifying.

That's what she did to him. She scared the hell out of him. And that was definitely a first. She asked nothing of him—another first—but gave everything. There were no questions, no ultimatums, no demands. She accepted each day as it came and went with an ease that amazed him.

He didn't know if he should be relieved or angry.

"I can take that." She reached for the basket when he moved beside her.

"With a forklift, maybe. What all do you have in here, anyway?"

She smiled at him, a mysterious, Mona Lisa smile. "All the baskets are secret. Only the highest bidder is entitled to uncover the contents."

She'd scooted him out of the kitchen at least half a dozen times this morning when she'd been cooking. The aromas that had drifted into the house had set his mouth watering, but then, so had the sight of her wearing an apron over a white T-shirt and shorts. He'd battled with himself between taking her right there on the kitchen table or snatching whatever smelled so good and making a run for it. The boys chattering on about the carnival had stopped him on the first issue, and Kasey's wooden spoon had stopped him on the second.

He was definitely a frustrated man.

"Come *onnnn*," Cody and Troy whined from the entrance. "You guys are slowpokes."

Two rides on the Tilt-A-Whirl, three on the bumper cars, and four roller-coaster rides later Cody and Troy were just getting warmed up and Slater felt as if he'd been thrown from a bronc, stomped on, then dragged around the ring six times. Kasey was finishing up her shift on the milk can toss when Slater staggered back with the boys.

"Slater took us on the roller coaster!" Troy told his mother.

Kasey smiled as she reached into the bright orange game apron she wore and pulled out three baseballs for a tall, reed-thin teenage boy wearing a baseball cap backward. "Did he?"

"Four times!" Cody added with delight.

"Four. My, my." Kasey noted the ashen tint to Slater's face and the distinct brownish red smudges on her sons' cheeks. "Was that before or after the chili dogs?"

"Before," Cody answered. "He took us on the Tilt-A-Whirl after."

She lifted her brows and glanced at Slater, who closed his eyes in painful memory and seemed to grow a shade paler. "Shall I call an ambulance?" she asked sweetly.

"Too late," he mumbled, sagging against the tent pole. "Just keep my funeral simple."

Shaking her head with amusement, she pulled off her apron and handed it to a blond waif with braces making eyes at the teenage boy who had already blasted unsuccessfully through his first three throws.

"Can we have some quarters and go to the fun house with Brian and his mom?" Cody asked. "They're waiting for us at the dime toss."

She was reaching into her pocket when Slater slipped

his hand behind Cody's ear and seemingly pulled out four quarters, then did the same to Troy. Their mouths dropped open and their eyes bugged.

"Wow! Mom, did you see that? Was that cool?" Cody said, and stared at the quarters now in his palm. Troy reached behind his own ear, then stared at Cody's, as if looking for a hole. "Wait till we tell Brian what Slater can do!"

They were off then, like two little arrows, straight for the dime toss three booths down. Sandy, Brian's mother, waved at Kasey and smiled, then hollered over that she'd keep them the rest of the afternoon.

"You know they'll hound you till you teach them that trick." She watched her sons talking to Brian, then pointing at Slater.

"An illusionist loses his powers if he reveals his secrets." Slater waved his hands mysteriously in front of her face, then pulled a white plastic daisy from thin air and handed it to her with a waggle of his eyebrows. "It squirts water, too."

She rolled her eyes at his antics, then stuck the thick rubbery stem of the flower into her hair right over her ear.

They strolled through the game booths, winning a purple elephant at the dart throw that cost Slater a lot more to win than it would have cost to buy. When he handed it to a pixie-faced toddler who'd been walking by with her big brother, the little mop-haired girl hugged the stuffed animal and beamed with delight.

What a shame he'd never had children, Kasey thought sadly. He'd been wonderful with the boys, and though she knew he wasn't aware of it and that he'd never admit it if he was, his eyes brightened every time he saw a baby. She could just picture him holding a newborn in those large hands of his, gently cradling the tiny bundle against his broad chest.

An ache spread through her as she realized that she hadn't pictured him holding just *his* baby, but *their* baby. She been careful to keep thoughts like that at bay, but each day he'd stayed had become more difficult not to want more, to want it all. All of him, with her and the boys, for the rest of their lives.

They hadn't discussed his leaving once, but she'd sensed something in him these past couple of days, the caged animal, pacing, wanting to be let out. To be let go. She knew in her heart that this day would be their last day together, that he'd be leaving tomorrow. She wanted to throw something, kick her feet, yell at him...beg him...

But she'd do nothing. Say nothing. The decision to stay had to be his. Tantrums and tears would only make it more difficult. She didn't want that between them when he left. She wanted only the memory of his laugh when he roughhoused with the boys, the mischievous smile in his eyes when he was about to do something wicked and the feel of his body against hers when he made love to her.

Those were the things she would always have, the things she would always remember.

They were eating caramel apples when the wind suddenly picked up, batting balloons and banners everywhere, blowing napkins and papers in every direction. Slater put his arm around her, laughing as he shielded her from the flying dust, holding her close as he guided her around the corner of a tent.

They huddled beside a tent, waiting as the wind softened to a breeze. She wanted to stay like this forever, in the safety of his arms, with the strong steady beat of his heart against her cheek and the masculine scent that was his alone seeping into her very pores. He brushed his lips against the top of her head, whispering her name and she felt herself melt against him.

He stiffened suddenly and she glanced up at him, saw the hard narrowing of his eyes as he looked over her shoulder. She followed his gaze and saw his father in the fishing booth across the way, helping a little boy with thick glasses reel in a prize on his fishing pole. The youngster's face fell when he pulled up an empty hook. Jack told the boy to close his eyes and try again, and this time when they reeled it in, there was an action figure dangling on the end. The excited child tucked it in his palm and ran to show his mother, who smiled thankfully at Jack. Jack winked back and grinned.

"Go talk to him," Kasey said gently.

She felt the battle wage in Slater. His arms tightened around her shoulders, then dropped away. He stood there, his jaw hard, his gaze intense, and for one second she thought he might go.

But he didn't. Instead, he turned away. "I'll catch up with you in a little while," he said, pulling his hat low.

She sighed heavily, noticing the dark clouds billowing around the horizon as he walked away. A storm was coming, all right, she realized as a chill came over her. It was only a matter of time.

"Seventy dollah. I have seventy. Do I hear eighty? How 'bout eighty? Eighty dollah? Eighty, eighty, going once, going twice, *sold*—" the auctioneer's gavel slammed down on the table "—to the gentleman in the blue-striped shirt for eighty dollah. And a lucky man he is."

The man, Harland Willows, was not only lucky, Kasey

thought with a smile, he was smart, since his wife, Charlene, had made the basket. Rumor had it that Harland had been sleeping on the front porch swing since he'd come home late from Weber's Bar one night too many. But now, Charlene beamed proudly as she carried her basket to her husband and the crowd clapped at the generous bid, which was nearly double what the highest basket had already sold for. Kasey doubted that Harland would be sleeping on the swing tonight.

There were only two baskets left: her own and Millie Overby's, who had returned from her honeymoon yesterday. No one with even half a lick of sense would bid against her husband, Todd, who stood anxiously in the front row with his wallet in hand and a big moon-eyed grin on his face. The bidding was over quickly and the blushing bride joined her proud husband.

Kasey stood behind her own basket, her smile frozen on her face, her hands clasped stiffly in front of her as the auctioneer announced her name. She scanned the crowd, but there was no sign of Slater. She hadn't seen him since he'd walked away earlier, and the heaviness in her chest swelled up like a concrete balloon.

She hated this. Standing here like a fool, praying that someone, and at this point, *anyone*, would bid on her basket.

But what she really hated was how desperately she wanted that someone to be Slater.

Gritting her teeth, she stared straight ahead as the auctioneer lifted his hand to start the bidding. A knot twisted her stomach, and she chided herself mentally for being so silly, worrying about a stupid basket of food. So what if no one bid? She didn't have to take it personally, for heaven's sake.

"Thirty dollars!"

Kasey snapped her gaze to the masculine voice that boomed out the first bid. It was Steven Macklin, from the post office. A mixture of relief and disappointment swept through her as the auctioneer ran with the bid. At least she wouldn't be without a bid at all.

"Forty!"

Forty? She swiveled her glance to see Bobby Hackett grinning at her from the front of the crowd. When Billy Hackett raised the bid to forty-five, the brothers started to argue.

Her head was still spinning as the bids came in: MaryAnn's nephew, Simon Milbury, Jared Moss, the manager at the hay and feed, Marcus Finley, from the bait shop. She held her breath as Marcus held the highest bid at sixty-five dollars. Not Worm Boy, she thought with a nervous jump in her stomach. She couldn't eat lunch with a man who has his fingers in worms all day.

"One hundred dollars!"

The crowd cheered and clapped and Kasey's heart skipped a beat at the outrageous bid. Dumbfounded, she stared at the man who had shouted it.

Jim Burke.

She knew she should be flattered, and thrilled, that someone would buy her basket for such an exorbitant amount. Still, her heart sank and her throat felt thick as she watched Jim walk confidently toward her.

Damn you, Slater!

"One hundred dollah, folks. One hundred dollah, going once, going twice...going—"

"Two hundred dollars."

Her heart stopped completely this time and she forgot to breathe. The crowd gasped, then turned.

Slater stood at the back of the crowd, his expression hard as he stared at Jim. The determined glint in Slater's eyes challenged the cowboy to up the bid, but even Jim knew when it was time to drop the reins. With a tip of his hat, Jim smiled at Slater, then Kasey, and waved Slater on.

"Sold!" the auctioneer pounded his gavel. "To the benevolent bidder in the black Stetson!"

She watched him approach, heard the catcalls, saw the men slapping him on the back as he moved forward through the throng of people. Several single—and a few married—women stared at him with hungry eyes. Her cheeks burned as the crowd turned back to her with sly, knowing glances.

She'd wanted him to buy her basket, but not with bells and whistles and fireworks, for heaven's sake!

Ignoring them all, she stepped off the platform as Slater approached, shoved the basket at him, then turned and walked away.

What the hell was the matter with her? he thought, watching her storm off. Was she still mad because he'd left her by the fishing booth and gone off by himself for a few minutes? Dammit, he'd needed some time alone right then, that was all. It wasn't like her to get all fired up over something like that. He followed her around the corner of a tent on the outside of the carnival, ready to have it out with her, when she turned on him.

"Two hundred dollars! What the hell's the matter with you?"

Confused, he simply stared. "You're mad because I spent two hundred dollars?"

"You idiot." She jammed her hands on her hips. "You spent two hundred dollars on *me*."

Baffled, this time he said nothing.

She arched her head back and sighed. "In front of practically the entire town, Slater. The ad my boys placed has kept this town busy with gossip for two weeks. You buying my basket like that ought to keep them going for at least another six months.''

The basket made a cracking sound he held it so tight. ''Buying your basket like what?''

''Like one of the carnival sideshows. That price was more than twice what any other basket sold for, and that look you gave Jim Burke!''

He narrowed his eyes. ''What look?''

''You know what look.'' She leaned forward. ''Like you'd slain the saber-tooth and come to drag the woman back to your cave.''‘

''I did not.''

''You did, too.''

''Didn't''

''*Did.*'' She stabbed his chest with a finger.

He pressed his lips tightly together and glared at her. ''All right. So maybe I did. Maybe I didn't like the idea of that guy moving in so fast.''

''He's moving in with the same speed you're moving out, Slater. And what Jim does is my business—'' she stabbed at his chest again ''—not yours.''

This time he squeezed the basket so hard it did crack. And as much as he wanted to argue the point over what was his business and what wasn't, he knew he had no right. Instead, he slipped into another issue. ''Everyone's seen us together, Kasey, they all know we're old friends, that I'm just visiting for a few days. Why should the gossip be any more now than before?''

She closed her eyes on a groan. ''You know the saying, 'Better to keep your mouth closed and let them think you're stupid, than open it and remove all doubt'? That's what you've done. Removed all doubt.''

She was right, dammit. He realized she wasn't just

talking here about his stupidity. There'd be no doubt now in anyone's mind that there was more than friendship between Kasey and himself. But he'd heard all those men bidding on her—her basket—and when Jim Burke gave his bid, well, something just snapped and he'd doubled the price without thinking. He'd never meant to bring any bad talk to Kasey. He'd been as impulsive as he'd been stupid.

"Hey, Mom! Whatcha doing all the way over here?"

Cody and Troy ran up, with Brian and his mother several feet behind. "Can we go home with Brian now?" Cody asked. "His dad bought him Demon Dogs video game and we wanna go play."

"Sure you can." Kasey looked at Slater, then shifted her attention to her sons. "In fact, if it's all right with you, Sandy, I'd like to come along and watch."

Sandy glanced at Slater, who stared at empty space, then cleared her throat and looked back at Kasey. "Of course, it's all right."

"And Slater, too?" Troy asked excitedly.

"'Fraid not, sweetie. Slater's busy." She dropped one last wilting look at him. "Don't worry about me. I'll manage to find my way home when I'm ready. What a shame for you that you can't do the same."

She moved around him, chin up, and he knew there'd be no discussion. Especially in front of Sandy. He'd caused enough damage for one day.

Jaw tight, he watched them walk away, then stared down at the basket in his hand, afraid to open it. Something told him that what was inside was a big helping of crow.

The house was dark and Slater's truck nowhere in sight when Kasey returned home. In spite of the pep talk she'd given herself all afternoon, in spite of her vow to be strong, her heart sank as she stared at the lonely house and empty driveway.

"Thanks for the ride and company." Kasey forced a light tone to the voice as she slid out of the front seat of Sandy's Cherokee. "And thanks for keeping Cody and Troy tonight. Next weekend is definitely mine."

"I won't turn that down," Sandy said good-naturedly, then glanced at the house. "You okay?"

"Are you kidding? A quiet evening home alone? What could be better?" She desperately wished she could have talked her sons into coming home, but a night with Demon Dogs beat out a night with Mom anytime. "I'll swing by and pick them up in the morning."

"Not necessary. I'll drop them off on our way to see my folks in the morning." Sandy leaned across the front seat and looked at Kasey. "You sure you're all right?"

Kasey smiled this time. It had been a long time since she'd had a friend. Paul had discouraged friendships, and after the divorce, between working and the boys, there'd been no time. The few hours she and Sandy had spent together this afternoon they'd talked about girl stuff, laughed over the silly things their kids said and did and cautiously shared a few, nonprivate pieces of their lives. It was the beginning of a friendship, Kasey realized, a real friendship, and it felt good.

"I'm fine, Sandy. Really," she said, and this time she meant it. "Call if you have any problems or if you change your mind and you and Tom want to go out tonight to a late movie or dinner. You can bring the boys here."

"You must be joking." Sandy laughed. "Who do you think my husband really bought that video game for? The only problem I'll have is making him share with the boys.''

Smiling, Kasey closed the door and waved goodbye, then sighed heavily as she walked up the steps. Brownies, she decided. She'd make brownies. Not the regular kind, but the kind with cheesecake inside and chocolate on top. Lots of chocolate.

She opened the front door, and her heart stopped at the strange flickering coming from the living room, terrified for one moment that there might be a fire. But it wasn't a fire, she realized as she moved into the living room.

Candles. Four votives, flaming brightly beside each china place setting laid out on a white linen tablecloth that was spread out on the floor. Pink roses spilled from a silver vase. Cloth napkins folded inside crystal goblets. Mozart playing softly from a portable tape player.

Everything—except for the roses—that she'd packed in her picnic basket.

Heart pounding heavily, she turned as he came out of the kitchen, hot pads in hand, carrying chicken scallopini in one bowl and garlic mashed potatoes in another. Both dishes she'd made that morning and had kept on ice in the basket. They were steaming now, obviously just taken right out of the oven.

''Oh, good, you're just in time,'' he said casually, moving past her. ''Tell the boys to get washed up and come get it while it's hot.''

''The boys are at Brian's.'' She stared at him, watching as he set the bowls down on the fireplace hearth.

''Oh.'' He sounded disappointed. ''Well, I don't have to feel guilty about already eating those cheesy puffy things, then. I got started on those and couldn't stop.''

He slapped his hands together then and sat cross-legged on the floor in front of a plate. "Let's eat."

"Slater." Kasey moved carefully into the living room. "What is all this?"

"Looks like mashed potatoes and—" he leaned forward and sniffed at the scallopini "—chicken, right?"

She frowned at him. "That's not what I mean and you know it."

"Sit down." He waved a hand at the place setting beside him. "Please."

Uncertainly, she knelt. He took her hand, then ran his thumb over the backs of her fingers. She struggled to ignore the tingle that danced up her arm.

"I'm not good at apologies," he said, then drew in a deep breath. "I'm sorry I bought your basket."

Some apology! Teeth clenched, she tried to yank her hand from his.

"I didn't mean it that way." He shook his head and held on tightly to her hand. "What I meant was, I'm sorry I made a spectacle like I did. I was out of line and well, I acted like a...a—"

"Jerk?" she offered. "Caveman?"

He winced. "You're not going to make this easy, are you?"

"Not a chance."

He reached for a knife and handed it to her, pointing the tip toward himself. "Go ahead. Make it quick."

"With a butter knife?" She ignored the twitch at the corner of her mouth. "And that's white linen you're eating on. Have you any idea how difficult it will be to get blood out of the tablecloth?"

"Does that mean a reprieve?"

Shadows from the candle flames flickered on his face. He stroked her hand, his expression soulful, his tone remorseful. Damn, but she hated him being so tender like this, so gentle and sincere.

But what she really hated was the longing she felt, the foolish hope that went so much deeper, and meant so much more than a picnic basket or what the town might think of her.

Her gaze swept the scene he'd laid out; the china, the candles, the flowers. The last of her defenses crumbled. "Roses," she murmured, and reached out to stroke one velvety petal. "They're beautiful."

He pulled her hand to his lips. "You're beautiful, Kasey. It staggers me how much."

He really meant it, she realized in stunned amazement. No man had ever looked at her like this before, certainly not Paul, and the desire she saw in Slater's eyes, the passion, made her feel beautiful. Tears gathered at the back of her throat, and the crack in her heart widened.

His lips nibbled on the sensitive skin of her palm, a tickling, erotic sensation that sent waves of pleasure rolling through her. Breath held, she leaned toward him.

"So you liked the cheese puffs?" Her voice wavered as she struggled to hold on to the last thread of sanity.

She felt his smile against her hand, then the hot, wet slide of his tongue over her palm to her wrist.

"Almost as much as the dessert," he muttered, working his way slowly up her arm.

She hesitated. She'd made cream puffs stuffed with whipped cream and drizzled with chocolate. "You ate the dessert first?"

"Of course not." He slipped one hand around her waist, pulling her closer as he nipped at the inside of her elbow. "I ate the cheesy puffy things first, then the dessert."

Her breath caught when his lips moved to her shoulder,

then she couldn't breathe at all when he nibbled at her neck.

"You're supposed to eat dessert last," she said weakly, letting her head fall back as his mouth explored the curve of her throat.

"Life's too short," he whispered roughly. "Too damn short."

He covered her mouth with his, and the soft whimper that escaped her parted lips was as much anguish as it was pleasure. Her heart ached from the love she felt for him, from knowing that their time was short and that he would be leaving soon. Memories would be all she'd have left, and she would carry them with her always, in her heart, in her soul.

An urgency filled her, and she wrapped her arms around him, desperately needing him, needing to be closer, to be a part of him. She breathed in the scent of him, the masculine scent that was his alone, felt the hard press of his body against hers, the deep, hot thrust of his tongue as he deepened the kiss. This was the man she loved, and for this moment he belonged only to her.

He'd wanted only to please her. There'd been no seduction planned tonight, no intention of lovemaking. He'd envisioned Cody and Troy, Kasey and himself, sitting cross-legged around the "table" he'd set, all of them together, laughing, talking, sharing the day they'd had. It was almost as if he'd come to think of them as his *family*, and he'd paced endlessly from the kitchen to the front window, lonely for them, watching for Sandy's car, stopping himself half a dozen times from driving over to Brian's house and bringing them all back.

Gently he lowered her to the floor, grabbing a throw pillow from the sofa and tucking it under her head. Candlelight flickered like golden sparkles in her hair and lit the green of her eyes.

"I was afraid you wouldn't talk to me," he said, testing the waters of honesty.

She smiled softly and cupped his face with her fingers. "I was afraid you'd left."

Surprised, he stared down at her. "You thought I'd leave without saying goodbye to you or the boys?"

"I'm sorry."

"No." He frowned at her. "I'm the one who's sorry. If I've made you feel that way, then I have acted like a jerk. I wouldn't do that, Kasey."

"I know." Her fingers traced the outline of his mouth. "Fear is not always rational."

He laughed softly. "I don't think I've had a rational thought since I sat in Digger Jones's diner and read that ad your sons placed in the *Granite Ridge Gazette.*"

She lifted one brow. "Hugh Slater, are you telling me that you subscribe to the *Gazette?*"

Damn his loose tongue. He'd managed to avoid that little bit of information all this time, and now he spilled it out like a bucket of overturned marbles. He sighed inwardly. What the hell.

"Other than an eight-month stint I did in Venezuela, yes, I did keep my subscription. Just to sort of…keep up with things."

He waited for the speech, for the explication of how much a part of Granite Ridge he truly was, and how he belonged here. That he cared much more than he'd ever admit.

She knew all those things, he could see it in her eyes. But she said nothing, just held his gaze, her smile soft and sad, her touch on his face gentle.

"Make love to me, Slater."

Her words took his breath away, shook him to his very core. Once again, she'd caught him off guard, done the unexpected. He knew a life with her would never be boring, that surprises would be endless. Exciting.

And for one moment, one second of irrational thought, he wondered what that would be like. Wondered about things he'd never let himself wonder about before. Things he'd always thought were for the other guy. Having his own family, his own home, a wife who loved him.

Was it possible?

And then she pulled him to her, pressed her lips to his, and his thoughts scattered like leaves in the wind. He thought only of her, of the tender touch of her hands on his face, the soft brush of her mouth against his. He lost himself to her, fell into that place where time ceased to exist and there was only Kasey. He breathed her scent, something exotic and floral, tasted the sweetness of her lips, a taste of extravagant dark wine, felt the soothing touch of her hands, like a silk scarf sliding over his skin.

He wanted to be gentle, to be tender, but a beast rose in him, a need so strong, so fierce that he lost control at her soft plea. With a groan, he pulled her underneath him, slanting his mouth against hers, kissing her hard, forcing her lips to open wider for him, insisting that her tongue meet his, needing her to be as wild for him as he was for her.

And she was. She moaned deeply, wrapping her arms tightly around his neck, arching her body up, offering herself. He took everything she offered and it wasn't enough. It wasn't enough.

He pulled away from her suddenly, rising to his knees, straddling her, holding her passion-filled gaze with his as he unsnapped his jeans. Her eyes darkened, her breath quickened as she watched him. The hiss of metal heightened the anticipation. His gaze never left hers, not when he hauled the denim from his hips, not when he slid her dress upward.

Her chin lifted, and she caught her bottom lip when he slid one finger under the lace edge of her panties. She made a soft sound as he explored the hot sweetness of her body, moving gently back and forth, until she moaned and writhed under his touch.

"Slater," she whispered hoarsely, "please. Now."

Slowly he tugged her panties away, following in their wake with his lips, kissing every inch of her long, silky legs. He rose over her again, moving between her legs, unbuttoning the top of her dress as he kissed her cheek, her eyes, her chin, unhooking the front clasp of her bra, then kissing the rosy tip of each beautiful breast.

Her nipple beaded instantly under the hot, moist caress of his tongue and lips. She rose upward to him, digging her fingernails into his shoulders, his scalp, murmuring his name, swearing softly when he refused to hurry.

But when her hands moved downward, guiding, encouraging, stroking him, he could stand it no more. On a curse, he entered her roughly, deeply, thrusting into her even as she rose to meet him. The need between them was as raw, as consuming, as it was wild.

She cried out, and when the satiny glove of her body tightened fiercely around him, he went over the edge. He shuddered into her, again and again, his groan primitive and savage, a possessive sound of complete male satisfaction.

Gathering her in his arms, he rolled her on top of him to protect her from the hardwood floor, then reached for an afghan on the edge of the couch and threw it over them. She lay like a rag doll, her head on his chest, her body draped over his. The rapid beating of her heart matched his, and as it calmed, he might have thought her asleep except for the gentle brushing of her fingertips on his chest.

The music tape he'd been playing had stopped, two of the candles had gone out and the food was cold. Smiling, he pressed his lips to her forehead and let himself drift off.

Eleven

Slater stepped out of the shower, scrubbing at his chest and dripping hair with a towel as he sang his own version of Clint Black's "A Good Run of Bad Luck." His deep voice cut through the heavy steam in the small bathroom, and he opened the door into the bedroom, letting some of the mist escape, not to mention a few misplaced notes and incorrect verses.

Cody and Troy would be home soon, and he pulled his clothes on quickly, hoping for a few minutes alone with Kasey. She'd already dressed and gone down to the kitchen before he showered, and his stomach hoped she was in the mood to cook.

Better yet, he thought on a whim, he'd take her and the boys into town for breakfast. He'd had a hankering for some time now for a big plate of Callie's blueberry waffles. Ten years to be exact. And ten years' worth of hankering was enough to make a man turn a want into a need, a need so strong he thought he just might die if he didn't get it.

The phone rang when he was halfway down the stairs. He heard Kasey's pleasant hello after the second ring, then a moment later, "Oh, good morning, Jim."

He froze at the bottom of the steps, then walked stiffly to the kitchen door. Her back was to him, and she was bent over the end of the counter, writing on a notepad.

Her feet were bare under her snug-fitting jeans, her cotton top loose and falling over one shoulder, exposing that curve of skin he'd kissed no more than thirty minutes ago. She looked sexy as hell, and the fact that she was talking to Jim Burke irritated him no end. He heard her ask about a horse, and realized they were talking about that stallion Jim had for stud. But suddenly the topic of their conversation felt intimate to him, personal, and his irritation only built.

"I'll try and come by later, then," she was saying. "Maybe in the afternoon?"

Slater's jaw tightened hard enough to crack a tooth by the time she hung up. She turned then, smiling brightly at him. Her smile faded as she realized he'd heard her phone call.

"All right, Slater." With a sigh, she folded her arms and leaned back against the counter. "Let's get it over with."

He strode to the coffeepot and poured himself a cup. "I don't know what you're talking about."

She laughed dryly. "Right. And mules have babies."

He frowned at her comparison. "All right. So I don't like you talking to Jim. It bugs me, okay?"

"No, it's not okay. Jim and I are talking about a horse, and I might be doing business with him."

He didn't want to think about what she might be doing with him. "Have you seen this horse?"

She shook her head. "I'll take a look at him later."

"I'll come along. It's been a few years, but I still know good horseflesh. I'll just make sure that Jim isn't taking advantage of you." In more ways than one.

Kasey looked at him for a long time, then said very carefully, "Jim doesn't own the horse. He just works for the man who does."

Why had her voice dropped? he wondered. And why was she staring at him so seriously? "Fine. It doesn't matter. I can still give an opinion on the horse, no matter who owns it."

She drew in a slow breath, then said quietly. "Your father owns it."

He couldn't breathe for a moment, as if he'd been poleaxed. He stared back at her, unblinking. "You're doing business with my father?"

"We haven't signed a contract, but his fees are within my price range, and everyone knows your father breeds the best horses in a five-hundred-mile radius."

Anger warmed in the pit of his stomach. "Everyone knows he also charges the highest fees. Why is he suddenly so affordable to you?"

"I don't know why. I was his only daughter's best friend. Maybe he's trying to help me out. Is there something wrong with that?"

His anger grew hotter. "You also happen to be sleeping with his only son," he said crudely. "Maybe he thought he'd give you a special deal."

Shock registered clearly on her face. She straightened, her eyes glistening with hurt as she stared at him. "What's happened between you and me has nothing to do with your father."

"Everything in my life has to do with my father in one way or another. Everywhere I turn, even two thousand miles away, he's there, his voice calm, his eyes cold, telling me my sister was dead, that he'd make the arrangements and let me know. He'd let me know!" He slammed his coffee cup down on the counter and the hot black liquid sloshed over the sides. "He went back to work then, said, 'Oh, by the way, your sister is dead, and there's a broken water valve in the east pasture. Order the part.'"

"Everyone has to handle grief their own way. Your father chose to shut it out. You chose to run. You left Granite Ridge because it hurt too much to stay, to care about anything or anybody, most especially your father. If you weren't so damn pigheaded, you just might realize that."

"The only thing I realize," he said coldly, "is that I made one hell of a mistake coming here, thinking that you might need my help."

"I didn't ask you to come here," she said, her voice shaking. "I was doing fine before you showed up. I'll do fine after you leave."

She didn't need him, he thought, and the realization was like a knife in his gut. She'd never once even asked him to stay. Somewhere deep down, a tiny voice tried to catch his attention and tell him to be quiet, that he'd be sorry, but anger was the louder voice. "Oh, I'll be leaving all right. Just tell me this, did you go to him? Tell him you'd get me to hang around for a while and throw in a few good words for him?"

Her intake of breath was as sharp as if he'd struck her. He could almost see her recoil from him, then a curtain dropped over her eyes, closing off her emotions from him, leaving only a blank, hard expression as she leveled her gaze on his.

"Cody and Troy are on their way home," she said, each word carved from ice. "I'm going out to the barn. Please say goodbye to them and be gone before I come back."

Even in her bare feet, she reminded him of a haughty queen as she turned from him and moved across the kitchen, picking up her socks and boots, then quietly closing the back door behind her. His hands clenched into fists and without thinking he kicked a kitchen chair, sending it crashing sideways across the floor.

His father. All this time she'd been making a deal with him and she'd never said a word, letting him think it was Jim Burke that owned the horse. Dammit! He kicked the chair again. He should have realized it. All that talk about how his father had changed, about forgiveness. Well, he hadn't changed one little bit. He was still a manipulating bastard, using his power and money to control people. And the fact that he'd used Kasey to be a part of that only sank the knife in deeper. And she'd let him.

He heard the sound of a car pulling up and realized that the boys were home. He drew in a deep breath, reining his anger in, not wanting Cody and Troy to pay for his stupidity.

He stared at the framed picture on the wall, the one that said, Home Is Where The Heart Is. She wanted him gone, well, fine. He'd be gone, all right. In fact, he couldn't wait to get the hell out of here and hit the road. And as soon as he said goodbye to the boys, that's exactly where he intended to be. On the road to Alaska.

She waited until long after she'd fed the animals, long after she'd cleaned the stalls, then even longer after she heard the roar of Slater's truck driving away. But when she heard the sound of her sons calling her, she knew she could wait no more. Each step back to the house was like pulling her feet out of mud. Her legs and arms were heavy, her chest tight, her brain lost somewhere in a thick fog. She welcomed the numbness, knowing that when it wore off, there would be only pain.

Cody and Troy met her halfway, but they, too, moved with less enthusiasm, their faces somber and lifeless. She knew that Slater had said goodbye to them, and they, too, were having to deal with their own sorrow.

That realization sparked a defense in her, and she shook off the cloud surrounding her, refusing to let her sons suffer any more than they already had. She'd handle the pain later, but now, all that mattered was Cody and Troy.

Smiling, she hugged them both, then slipped an arm around each of them as they walked back to the house. "Hey, you boys hungry for lunch? How 'bout we cook up some chili dogs and macaroni and cheese?"

They shook their heads. "We had pancakes and bacon at Brian's house," Cody said quietly.

"We could drive into town for a sundae at the ice cream store." Kasey was grasping now, desperate to cheer her sons up.

"Slater's gone," Troy said.

"I know, sweetie." She pulled him closer to her.

"He said he'll call and write us letters." Cody leaned in close to her, too.

"Then he will," she said. "Won't that be great? Postcards from Alaska? No other kids at school will have those."

"I guess so." Cody kicked at a rock, which Troy immediately went after and stuck into his pocket.

What a fool she'd been. Slater had called himself an illusionist. She realized now that's what these past weeks had been. An illusion. A fantasy she'd desperately wanted to be real, but was nothing more than smoke and mirrors and disappearing quarters.

Heads hanging, Cody and Troy followed her into the house.

"Go on up and change your T-shirts," she told them brightly. "We'll go into town and after ice cream we'll go play some video games at the pizza parlor."

"Savage Jungle?" Cody asked.

It was a video game that she'd always forbidden them to play because it was violent. Maybe a little violence would do them all good today, she decided. "Sure. I'll even play, too."

A flicker of excitement lit their eyes, but still, they walked up the stairs, instead of their normal gallop when they were getting ready to do something fun.

Damn Hugh Slater! Kasey ground her teeth together. Her own misery she could stand, but to see her sons like this made her furious. And as she thought about what he'd said to her, his implication that she made some kind of a deal with his father, that fury turned into a white-hot rage.

Spotting the jigsaw puzzle on the coffee table behind her, she whirled suddenly and swept her arm across the tabletop. She watched the pieces fly, bouncing off the wall, skipping across the floor, hundreds of tiny bits of colorful cardboard. That was her life, she thought with a silent scream.

She stared at the mess, at each jagged piece scattered across the floor, then drew in a deep, calming breath and bent to pick each and every one up.

*   *   *

Marty Thompson waved at Slater and honked from his hay truck as they passed each other on the highway one mile outside of town. Slater raised a stiff hand in greeting, but there was no smile on his face, no enthusiasm behind the gesture. Just an empty, dull ache deep in his chest.

Hands tight on the steering wheel, he glanced down at the going-away presents on the seat beside him, both wrapped in brown paper lunch bags and tied with blue string. Cody and Troy had made him promise not to open them until later, but he'd found his gaze traveling repeatedly to the paper bags, wondering what was inside.

Neither boy had looked him in the eye as they'd shaken hands, or even when he'd impulsively pulled them both into his arms and hugged them tightly. But he'd felt them press against him, holding on to him as they buried their faces in his chest, eyes blinking furiously and lips working to hold back a sob.

He'd never dreamed saying goodbye would be so damn hard.

He'd nearly stomped out to the barn at least a dozen times before he left, needing to yell some more, to at least hear what she had to say for herself.

Needing to pull her into his arms and tell her he loved her.

What irony, he thought with a dry, short laugh. To realize now that he loved her.

All he could see was the hurt in her eyes, the pain he'd caused her when he'd accused her of conspiring against him with his father. He'd done and said some pretty nasty things in his life, but that one topped the cake.

Is this where his anger had brought him? To hurting everyone he loved or cared about? Kasey's words echoed in his head...*you left here because it hurt too much to stay, to care about anything or anybody....*

Cows from the Hopkins Ranch grazed close to the highway, and when he passed the Montgomery farm, Granite Ridge was merely a speck in his rearview mirror. Soon he knew it would disappear completely.

He could reach Amarillo by nighttime. If the roads were clear, sooner. Another four or five days of hard driving, he just might even get to Alaska. He didn't give a damn about sleeping or eating, anyway. He'd just go on the minimum until he got to Anchorage, then he could sleep for three days straight before he started work.

Settling back in his seat, his gaze slid once again to the paper bags beside him. He'd send them a postcard before he got to Alaska, he decided. No reason he had to wait. Hell, he might even call, though Kasey would answer and that would be awkward. But the thought of hearing her voice, even cold and distant, brought an immediate shifting in his gut.

Dammit to hell.

He kept driving, eyes narrowed, foot held firmly down on the accelerator, concentrating on the road. Up ahead was the Anderson place, then Ralph Weston's ranch, and then—

He slowed the truck, nearly screeching to a stop at the turnoff for the cemetery and stared at the long, carefully manicured driveway leading into the place where Jeanie and his mother were buried.

Why hadn't he come here before? he asked himself. He'd been in town more than two weeks and not once had he even thought about it.

You left here because you hurt too damn much to stay, to care about anything or anybody....

A car honked and swerved around him, and still he sat in the middle of the road.

Palms sweating, heart pounding, he turned his truck and drove like a wooden puppet down the asphalt-paved entrance. He followed the road, but it felt as if someone else had taken the steering wheel and he was a passenger, and when the truck stopped, it stopped only a feet away from the Slater family plots.

He left the truck door open when he slid out. The graves were impeccably cared for, and two rosebushes, red for his mother, pink for his sister, bloomed profusely over each headstone, their sweet fragrance filling the warm afternoon air.

There'd been no rosebushes ten years ago. He glanced around the cemetery. None of the other graves had them, either. Someone had obviously planted them.

Kneeling between the graves of the only other two women he'd ever loved besides Kasey, Slater realized that he was holding Cody and Troy's gifts in his hand. He opened Cody's first, smiled at the stack of baseball cards inside. He opened Troy's next, then had to swallow back the lump in his throat. Rocks. Simple pieces of granite and slate, some sharp and jagged, some smooth, but each one held a special meaning for Troy. A memory.

"Hugh."

He stood at the sound of his name, turned to see his father standing a few feet away with two small bouquets in his hand, one red carnations, the other pink. "Dad. I...I didn't hear you drive up."

His father hesitated, then moved closer. Slater watched him, noticing with more awareness now the cautious measure of his gait.

"I come here after church on Sunday."

Slater gestured to the rosebushes. "You do this?"

Jack knelt slowly, painfully, slipping the bouquets into the metal vases at the headstones, then carefully arranging each flower. "I put them in after I got out of the hospital, just in case, well—"

He hesitated, and Slater stared at the man as if he were seeing him for the first time, not just in ten years, but in his whole life. "In case you couldn't come here anymore."

He stared up at the clear blue sky, then glanced around at the willows surrounding the stretch of green lawn. "Couldn't hardly bring them flowers if I was lying beside them. This way I could be sure."

Jack's brow knotted in pain as he straightened his knees and stood. He pulled a pair of clippers from his back pocket and began to snip the wilted roses from the bushes. Slater stared at his father's hands. Rough, weathered hands that had worked the land for more than sixty years.

And those same hands, hands that had disciplined with a vengeance, hands that had taught with persistent determination, now planted and tended rosebushes with loving care.

A battle waged within Slater; the son that wanted to strike out, to blame, and the son—the son he'd thought long dead—that wanted to console.

"I blamed you," Slater said. It wasn't an accusation, nor was it vindication. It was simply a matter of fact.

"I failed you both." Jack ran his hand over one pink carnation. "Jeanie in the worst possible way."

Why did those words bring no satisfaction? Slater wondered. Isn't that what he'd always wanted to hear? An admission of some kind, any kind, from his father? An acknowledgement that he'd cared about more than his damn ranch?

A weariness crept over him. Ten years' worth. "I failed her, too. We could have stopped her."

Jack shook his head. "She was seventeen and in love for the first time in her life. There's no stopping a woman in love. They tried with your mama, you know."

Slater watched his father trim a brown leaf from the bush. "You and Mom?"

"I was a cowboy, a drifter. She was the most beautiful woman ever lived. Folks told her I'd never amount to anything, I'd leave her penniless, with a passel of good-for-nothing brats." He leaned forward and breathed in the scent of one red rose. "We were eighteen when we ran off."

That's why his father was so driven all those years, Slater realized. Why he'd worked so damn hard, why money was so important to him. And why he'd expected excellence from his children. He'd needed to prove something, not only to all those people, but to his wife and to himself.

"It scared me how much I loved your mama. I think that's why I hardly ever told her. I never really thought I deserved her and you kids. Deep down I always thought I would lose it all, just like everyone said."

He moved to the pink rosebush and touched one velvety petal of a bud. "I guess they were right."

It wasn't going to be an easy road, Slater knew, nor was it going to be smooth, but it was time to change direction, time to come back to the place he'd been running from for ten years.

Time to come home.

"No, Dad," Slater said quietly, and held out his hand. "They weren't right. You have me."

Jack looked at his son's offered hand, then glanced up in disbelief. Slater saw a light flicker in those dark, tired eyes, then cautiously he reached out, fingers shaking, and slipped his hand into his son's.

His father's grip was firm, his thick-knuckled hand strong and calloused. They stared at each other, neither one wanting to let go, then suddenly, with a loud laugh, clasped their arms around each other.

A breeze picked up as they hugged. Leaves rustled on the nearby trees. The scent of roses filled the air.

When Slater stood back, he didn't try to hide the moisture burning his eyes. Neither did his father. They simply stared at each other and smiled.

"Alaska, huh?" Jack shook his head. "You never liked the cold much, son."

Slater laughed. "So I've been told." Slater tipped back his hat. "Now you want to tell me about this horse I heard put a dent in that hard-hat skull of yours?"

"Hey, Kasey, glad you could make it. Be with you in a minute."

Jim Burke sat on the back of a beautiful chestnut stallion and waved at her as she parked her truck beside the corral. He turned his attention back to a cluster of cows that had scattered to the far end of the enclosure, then swung the horse around and lit out after them.

Cody and Troy tumbled out of the truck behind her, watching in awe as Jim slowed the horse, then, like a practiced dance, man and horse worked together to single out one cow and sever it from its companions. Three other men clapped and cheered when the cattle dispersed and one poor animal was left standing alone, trapped by the team of horse and rider.

"That was cool!" Cody said, moving closer to the corral. Troy followed his brother and both boys hung on the pipe fencing, their eyes wide with fascination as Jim whirled the horse around and went after the next poor victim.

Kasey smiled softly as she watched her sons. It was the first sign of life she'd seen in them all day. They'd gone to town as she'd promised, but even ice cream and video games hadn't really interested them, not even Savage Jungle. They'd simply gone through the motions like little robots, but with no real enthusiasm.

Like herself.

You also happen to be sleeping with his only son.... Maybe he thought he'd give you a special deal.

Slater's words played like a broken record in her mind, over and over. She could still see the fury in his eyes, hear the anger in his voice. He'd aimed his venom-tipped arrow well, she thought. That he could accuse her like that, imply such a horrible thing, had cut into her very soul.

She knew that it was all going to hit her later, like the delayed blast of an explosion. But she'd choose her time to grieve, a time when she could be alone and allow herself to release the pain and anger bottled up inside her. Her sons needed her now. They needed her strength and love, needed to know that she was the one person who would never, ever leave them.

"What do you think of him?"

Startled from her thoughts, Kasey turned abruptly and stared into familiar dark brown eyes. The cinch around her heart tightened as Jack Slater nodded at her. She forced a smile back.

"The horse is beautiful." She assumed Jack meant the chestnut and not Jim. What she didn't need was any more matchmaking.

"Thought you might like him."

She hesitated, frowning as she looked at the magnificent horse, then back to Jack. "You can't possibly be saying that this is the stud for my horse."

"Yep. That's him, all right."

It couldn't be, she thought wildly. A horse like this, a horse this incredible, was way out of her price range.

She had to clear her voice before she could speak. "Mr. Slater, I could never afford this horse. Maybe in a couple of years, but not now."

"Call me Jack." He whistled at Jim, who reined in the stallion and headed for the barn. "Go on up to the house and make yourself comfortable. I'll be there shortly."

"But—"

"Go on now," he said sternly. "I want to show your young'uns what it feels like to ride on a champion cutting horse."

Cody and Troy yelled with excitement, then ran for the barn. "Mr. Slater, Jack—"

He turned, waving her off as he walked away. "Don't you worry. I'll take good care of them."

She stood there, feeling abandoned for the second time that day. Sighing, she turned and walked to the house, then followed a round cheeked, silver haired housekeeper into Jack Slater's office.

She was too restless to sit in the worn leather chair the woman had offered, so Kasey paced the length of the oversize oak desk, nibbling on her fingernail. A wall of floor-to-ceiling windows overlooked the paddock, and the wall to her left hosted hundreds of awards and ribbons. She glanced at the wall behind her, and her heart slowed at the framed photographs. Family pictures. Slater's mother, Jeanie, Slater. There were dozens. School pictures, birthday parties, Christmas. Each snapshot a piece of their lives frozen on a piece of paper.

She moved closer, studying each one, feeling the moisture build in her eyes as she stared at the smiling face of her best friend, biting her lip as she recognized her own face in one picture taken at Jeanie's sixteenth birthday party. Eyes sparkling, they had their arms wrapped around each other, their mouths open with laughter. They were going to start a ranch together, Kasey remembered, swallowing the sob in her throat.

She touched the picture, smiling, letting the memories wash through her. How she still missed her, wondered what their lives would have been if only...

Her fingers slipped from the picture. Life was full of if-only's. And there was nothing to do but move on, keep going, even when your heart was broken and your dreams shattered.

And she would keep going, she vowed, but her brave words felt empty and false.

"That's my favorite," Kasey heard a deep voice say behind her. "That one and the one right above it."

She froze, then turned slowly, and stared at the man in the doorway.

Slater.

He moved beside her, reaching over her as he pulled the photograph from the wall. "Jeanie was only two here, I was nine. It was the Christmas before my mom died. The last time we were all together."

Heart pounding, she dragged her gaze from his face and looked at the picture. His mother sat under a brightly decorated Christmas tree, holding Jeanie in her arms, smiling at the camera. A very young, reed-thin Slater knelt in front of his father, who stood beside the tree, arms folded as he stared straight ahead.

"I got a bike that year," he said, smiling at the memory.

He replaced the picture, then drew in a deep breath and looked down at her. "Kasey, I'm sorry."

She just stared at him, shaken not only by the fact that he was actually standing here—in his father's house—but that he was apologizing to her.

When she didn't speak, he jammed his hands into his pockets. "Maybe if you'd just hit me or something," he offered. "Anything. Just say you'll forgive me."

She did think about hitting him, and wasn't completely certain she was ready to forgive. "What are you doing here?"

He walked to the windows and stared out, watching two ranch hands work a frisky yearling. "I got as far as the cemetery." He turned back to look at her. "Did you know my dad planted rosebushes?"

She nodded slowly, not certain what was happening here, afraid to even think about what might be happening here.

"Why didn't you tell me?"

"As I recall, every time I even mentioned your father, you were ready to bolt."

"Running is what I do best." He moved toward her, took her hand and sighed. "And the only thing that kept me going, kept me alive all those years, was my anger. I knew if I let it go that all I'd have left is pain, the realization that every person I ever loved, that loved me, was gone."

"Your father loves you," she said softly. "He always has. He just doesn't know how to show it."

"I seem to be having the same problem myself these days."

He gazed down at her, his eyes a richer, deeper brown than she'd ever remembered, his expression soft and tender. Sounds drifted in from outside: a ranch hand's whistle, the shrill whinny of a horse, the bawling of dis-gruntled cows. But here, in this office, the sound of her erratic heartbeat drowned them all out.

"I was on my way out of town," he said. "It didn't take me long to realize what an idiot I'd been, that I'd taken my frustration and anger at myself out on you. Then suddenly I was at the cemetery, and so was my dad. He had flowers for my mom and Jeanie." Slater smiled softly. "Well, we couldn't very well fight in front of them, could we? So we talked, maybe for the first time in our lives we really talked. All those years I just thought he didn't give a damn about me or Jeanie. But I realize now that he did care, just like you said, he just didn't know how to show it. After my mom died, he just sort of shut down, wouldn't let himself feel. It just hurt too damn much."

He took her hand and she felt a shiver run through her as he brought her fingers to his lips. "You were right, Kasey. I did the same thing after Jeanie died. I didn't want to hear it, but everything you said to me earlier was true. I didn't want to care about anything or anybody. Most especially you and Cody and Troy. The thought of losing you or the boys scared the hell out of me. It made me want to run again, like I've been doing for ten years."

"We're not going anywhere," she said quietly, tight-ening her fingers around his.

She saw the peace in his eyes now, a peace that had never been there before. It shone from deep inside, from a place he'd kept closed off for ten years. Jeanie would be so happy, Kasey realized. And his mom. She felt their presence here with them, and knew that Slater felt it, too.

He leaned forward to kiss her, then suddenly stepped away from her and cleared his throat.

"Oh, I almost forgot." He reached into his pocket and

pulled out a piece of folded paper. "I wanted to go over this new job application with you."

New job application? One second he's telling her how much he cares for her, the next he's talking about a job? Her sons might like roller coasters, but she couldn't take much more of this ride with Slater. "I thought you already had a job in Alaska," she said tightly.

"Jeez, Kasey, you know I can't stand the cold. I found another ad for a position that's much more to my liking. Only problem is, I don't have any experience."

She was torn between screaming at him and collapsing into a puddle of tears. Damn this man! How could he be so matter-of-fact and discuss job opportunities with her like this? Gritting her teeth, she stared blankly at him, silently enduring her misery.

He unfolded the paper and began to read, "'Dear Ms. Acacia Donovan Morgan. Recently I read your advertisement in the *Granite Ridge Gazette*. I am very interested in the position of husband and father, but am sorely lacking in the skills and qualifications. However, I am a fast learner and a hard worker.'"

Kasey couldn't breathe. She felt suddenly weak, and struggled to keep her legs from buckling under her.

He went on. "'I do like kids, especially two little pistols named Cody and Troy who deserve better than me, but I will strive to make myself worthy as a father and role model who will love them without question.'"

He paused and looked up at her. She simply stared at him, watching as he set the paper on the desk and held his eyes steady on hers.

"I am also inadequate in the skills required of a husband," he said evenly as he moved toward her, "but there is no job more important to me, no job I will work harder at, than the occupation of marriage. And the one qualification I have, the most important, is that I love you more than life itself. Please say you love me, too, and you'll marry me.''

Tears burned her eyes. She had to swallow moisture gathering in her throat, but she still couldn't speak. With a small sob, she flung herself at him, throwing her arms around his neck and her legs around his waist. Laughing, he spun her, then brought his mouth to hers and kissed her gently.

"Do you love me?'' he asked, never taking his lips from hers. "I need to hear you say it.''

"Of course I love you. I've always loved you, you big idiot.''

Hardly romantic words, but they brought a huge smile to his face. "And you'll marry me? Right now, today?''

"How about tomorrow?'' she whispered, brushing her lips to his. "A girl has to get herself ready, you know. I want to look perfect for you.''

"You are perfect. You always have been.'' He set her down, then reached into his jeans' pocket and pulled out a ring. "It was my mother's.'' He slipped it on her finger. "My dad gave it to me.''

"Your father's in on this, too?''

He grinned. "Knee deep. He's damn excited about finally having grandkids. Says he wants a least half a dozen more.''

It was impossible to stop the tears now. She stared at the sparkling solitaire on her finger, thinking her heart might burst from the happiness she felt.

"A half dozen, huh?'' She brought her lips to his again, kissed him deeply. "An ambitious man.''

"Like father, like son,'' he murmured against her mouth. "How 'bout we go tell the boys?''

Arms around each other, they walked to the barn. Jack

stood at the barn entrance with Cody and Troy, feeding carrots to the stallion.

"She said yes, Dad," Slater yelled, then scooped her up in his arms. She gasped as he swung her around. Jack's face broke into a grin as he watched them. Cody and Troy laughed at the sight of Slater with their mother, then ran over.

"Slater!" Both Cody and Troy hugged his legs. "Why did you come back?"

Slater set Kasey down, but still held her hand as he knelt in front of the boys. "Well, guys, you know that ad you placed..."

* * * * *

Watch for Barbara McCauley's
next sultry tale,
SEDUCTION OF THE RELUCTANT BRIDE,
coming May 1998 from Silhouette Desire.

SANDRA STEFFEN

**Continues the
twelve-book series—
36 Hours—in February 1998
with Book Eight**

MARRIAGE BY CONTRACT

Nurse Bethany Kent could think of only one man who could
make her dream come true: Dr. Tony Petrocelli, the man who
had helped her save the life of the infant she desperately
wanted to adopt. As husband and wife, they could provide the
abandoned baby with a loving home. But could they provide
each other with more than just a convenient marriage?

For Tony and Bethany and *all* the residents of Grand Springs,
Colorado, the storm-induced blackout was just the beginning
of 36 Hours that changed *everything!* You won't want to miss a
single book.

Available at your favorite retail outlet.

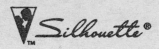

Take 4 bestselling love stories FREE

Plus get a FREE surprise gift!

Special Limited-time Offer

Mail to Silhouette Reader Service™

3010 Walden Avenue
P.O. Box 1867
Buffalo, N.Y. 14240-1867

YES! Please send me 4 free Silhouette Desire® novels and my free surprise gift. Then send me 6 brand-new novels every month, which I will receive months before they appear in bookstores. Bill me at the low price of $3.12 each plus 25¢ delivery and applicable sales tax, if any.* That's the complete price and a savings of over 10% off the cover prices—quite a bargain! I understand that accepting the books and gift places me under no obligation ever to buy any books. I can always return a shipment and cancel at any time. Even if I never buy another book from Silhouette, the 4 free books and the surprise gift are mine to keep forever.

225 SEN CF2R

Name	(PLEASE PRINT)	
Address		Apt. No.
City	State	Zip

This offer is limited to one order per household and not valid to present *Silhouette Desire*® subscribers. *Terms and prices are subject to change without notice.
Sales tax applicable in N.Y.

UDES-696   ©1990 Harlequin Enterprises Limited

Return to the Towers!

In March
New York Times bestselling author

NORA ROBERTS

brings us to the Calhouns' fabulous
Maine coast mansion and reveals the
tragic secrets hidden there for generations.

For all his degrees, Professor Max Quartermain has a
lot to learn about love—and luscious Lilah Calhoun is
just the woman to teach him. Ex-cop Holt Bradford is
as prickly as a thornbush—until Suzanna Calhoun's
special touch makes love blossom in his heart.
And all of them are caught in the race to solve
the generations-old mystery of a priceless
lost necklace…and a timeless love.

Lilah and Suzanna
THE Calhoun Women

**A special 2-in-1 edition containing
FOR THE LOVE OF LILAH and
SUZANNA'S SURRENDER**

Available at your favorite retail outlet.